DEADLY RANCH REFUGE

AMITY STEFFEN

Recycling programs for this product may not exist in your area.

ISBN-13: 978-1-335-95778-8

Deadly Ranch Refuge

For questions and comments about the quality of this book, please contact us at CustomerService@Harlequin.com.

Love Inspired
22 Adelaide St. West, 41st Floor
Toronto, Ontario M5H 4E3, Canada
www.LoveInspired.com

HarperCollins Publishers
Macken House, 39/40 Mayor Street Upper,
Dublin 1, D01 C9W8, Ireland
www.HarperCollins.com

Printed in Lithuania

Ella let out a little growl of frustration as she entered her personal space and looked around.

"It was silly of me to hope that just being in a familiar place would make my memory come rushing back."

She gasped when the window behind her shattered. Glass sprayed into the room. It took Jude only a split second to ascertain the cause.

"Pipe bomb!" he shouted, grabbing her by the arm and nearly yanking her off her feet.

He shoved Ella in front of him as they ran through the shop, toward the front door.

Please, God. Please, God. The simple plea played on a silent loop in Jude's mind as they raced toward safety. He trusted that the Lord knew exactly what he was asking, even if his mind couldn't finish forming a coherent prayer.

They reached the door and opened it, had barely touched the sidewalk when the bomb exploded.

A deafening sound filled the air. The building shook as Jude dived toward the sidewalk with Ella in his arms...

Amity Steffen lives in northern Minnesota with her two boys and two spoiled cats. She's a voracious reader and a novice baker. She enjoys watching her sons play baseball in the summer and would rather stay indoors in the winter. She's worked in the education field for more years than she cares to count, but writing has always been her passion. Amity loves connecting with readers, so please visit her at Facebook.com/amitysteffenauthor.

Books by Amity Steffen

Love Inspired Suspense

Reunion on the Run
Colorado Ambush
Big Sky Secrets
Missing in Montana
Deadly Ranch Refuge

Visit the Author Profile page at LoveInspired.com.

And thine ears shall hear a word behind thee,
saying, This is the way, walk ye in it, when ye turn
to the right hand, and when ye turn to the left.

—*Isaiah* 30:21

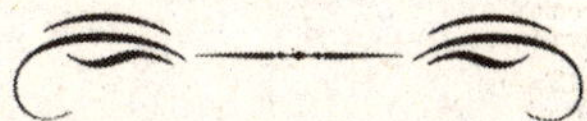

To my cousin Nikki, whose love of reading goes back as far as my own.

ONE

Jude Sheridan gripped the steering wheel and leaned forward in his seat. The windshield wipers were working valiantly at whisking away the sleet that was falling from the sky. Autumn in Haven Creek, Montana could be fickle. Last week had seen near record highs. Today, the roads were covered in a thin sheet of ice.

It was the sort of evening that begged a person to stay home, preferably with a roaring fire blazing. But Lexie, his younger sister, had called and she needed him. Her furnace was on the fritz again. Last time, he'd been able to tinker with it and get it going. That was his plan tonight. Get it fired up instead of calling the off-hours number and then have a professional look at it in the morning. If he couldn't get it going, he'd take Lexie back to his ranch.

He wasn't sure what had other people out on the road tonight. Especially the two vehicles coming toward him. The first was a car, and behind it, a much bigger truck. He only noticed because it appeared as if the truck was driving awfully close to the car. It seemed reckless considering how the smaller vehicle had started to fishtail.

Jude slowed his own truck, unsure of what trajectory the car was going to take. It began to slip and skid over the road, only to get its bearings and then slide around again.

"Slow down if you're struggling so much," Jude muttered to the driver.

But the driver didn't heed his warning. The car fishtailed, wildly this time, and Jude realized then just how close the truck was to the car's bumper. Close enough to hit the car? Ram it? That's sure what it looked like. But…why?

There was no time to contemplate that question. The old truck backed off and then backfired loudly. The car slid sideways. Had the driver of the truck rammed it? Or had the car's driver lost control due to the poor road conditions? Regardless, the result was the car careening wildly out of control as it came straight at him.

"Oh, God, help!" The plea was short, all he could muster in those crucial seconds, but he cried it out from the depths of his soul.

The small car flew toward him, sideways now, as he hit his own brakes. His truck slid as his grip on the steering wheel became ironclad.

The driver of the other truck floored the gas pedal and tore down in the ditch, where the big tires had traction in the grass, then flew past Jude and the oncoming car.

In the next instant, the car clipped Jude's bumper. For just a moment, he thought that would be it, that it would all turn out okay, but then the car ricocheted off his truck and slid sideways toward the ditch, where a tire caught the ridge between the asphalt and the earth. Before Jude could blink, the car flipped and rolled. Then rolled again.

He pulled his truck to the side of the road and leaped out, arms flailing and feet sliding around as he hit the slick, ice-glazed shoulder. He pulled his phone from his pocket as he ran toward the car that had just slammed into a tree. He dialed 911 as he raced toward the vehicle.

The operator came on after only two rings. "Nine-one-one. What's your emergency?"

"This is Game Warden Jude Sheridan," he said. "I just witnessed a car flip and roll. I'm approaching the car now, but please send an ambulance. The rollover occurred approximately three miles south of my house. My address is twenty-three twenty-one Sagebrush Bend."

His heartbeat kicked in his chest. He knew this car.

"Ella," he whispered, then shook his head. No, Ella had ended their engagement months ago. She had no reason to be out this way. There were probably a million silver Acuras on the road.

He reached the car, which had landed upright, though the top was crimped and the windshield had shattered in a spiderweb pattern. The driver's doorframe was bent, an airbag pressed up against it, blocking his view of the person inside.

Heedless of the emergency operator asking for more details, he dropped the phone to the ground. He needed to get that door open. Now. Had to see for himself who was inside. Regardless of whether or not it was Ella, he was sure medical aid would be necessary. As a game warden, he was trained in first aid and emergency response.

An ambulance was on the way, but it could be ten minutes or more before it arrived. An absolute lifetime in an emergency. A sickening smell hit his nostrils.

Gasoline.

A moment later, he heard the distinct hiss and crackle of a fire.

He lunged toward the door. It was locked. Of course, it was. He whirled and raced back toward his truck. His jack stand was in the truck bed. After grabbing it, he rushed back to the car. The flames were visible now, under the hood. Wasting no time, he flung the jack stand at the back passenger window of the Acura. The glass cracked but didn't break. He struck it again. And again. Every second felt like an eternity. When he'd finally created a hole big enough to stick his hand through, he managed to unlock the back door. He tugged it open, then reached forward to unlock the driver's door.

The airbag had deflated some by now, and was wilting into the driver's lap. When he leaned in, he had a clear view of long, raven-colored curls.

Ella. It was her. He had no doubt.

His heartbeat felt as if it went into overdrive.

He tugged the driver's door. Nothing happened. He pulled again. And again. Then braced one booted foot against the car and gave a tremendous yank as he begged God to let the door open. It opened with a sickening creak…but it opened.

"Ella! Ella, it's Jude! Can you hear me?" He kneeled beside her, noticing the enormous lump swelling near her temple. Instantly, he wondered about a back or neck injury. Yet he had no choice other than to move her. The fire was flickering through the creases in the rumpled hood. He may only have seconds before it began to creep through the floorboards.

Or worse. The car could explode.

Sirens wailed in the distance. His relief was short-lived because he knew they were still several minutes out.

Leaning in, he unbuckled Ella's seat belt. Then, as gently as if he was lifting an injured newborn, he scooped her from the car.

She moaned in his arms. Her eyelids fluttered but remained closed.

"You're going to be okay," he murmured, his mouth close to her ear. "You're going to be fine. Help is on the way."

He staggered toward his truck, then down into the ditch

on the opposite side, hoping to use his vehicle for protection should the Acura explode.

The thought of putting her on the hard, frozen ground gave him pause.

A cruiser came into view then, the first of the emergency vehicles to arrive. A wave of relief crashed over him as his friend, Officer Blake Thompson, leaped from the cruiser.

"The car's on fire!" Jude called.

Blake dove back into the cruiser and appeared again holding a fire extinguisher.

He raced toward the Acura as the ambulance arrived. A fire truck lumbered along in the distance.

Jude was only vaguely aware of Blake putting out the fire as he rushed toward the ambulance with Ella held close to his chest. A female first responder hurried toward him while a male opened the back doors of the ambulance. He tugged out a gurney.

"I'm Laura," the first responder said. "What do we have here?"

"Female. Twenty-eight." She was two years younger than him, too young to be facing a life and death situation, he thought before continuing. "She was in a rollover and hasn't gained consciousness. The airbag deployed. I had to pull her from the vehicle when it caught fire."

The male responder rushed toward them, pushing the gurney. Jude laid Ella onto it as gently as he could.

"Her name is Ella Clarke. I know her, though I'm not sure what she was doing out this way."

"My name's Colin," the male responder said. "We can take it from here."

Jude stood back, knowing it was best to let these two do their jobs.

The fire truck pulled up then, though from what Jude

could tell, Blake had already succeeded in putting out the fire. Jude was only vaguely aware of them. His attention was solely on Ella. The woman whom he had, not that long ago, considered the love of his life. Until she'd toyed with his heart, acting as if their relationship had been nothing but a game.

His head told him he should step away from this situation. He'd done everything he could possibly do. He'd done his civic duty and now, it was time to let the other professionals take over. That's what he should do.

Instead, he stepped forward, intent on getting some information.

A firm hand on his shoulder stopped him.

He whirled and came face-to-face with Blake.

"Is that Ella?" Blake asked, his expression showing his disbelief.

Jude raked a hand through his hair and nodded. "Yeah, it is."

"What happened?"

Jude told him everything from the moment he'd noticed the car slip, to when he was certain that the truck rammed the car's bumper.

"Any chance you got the plate number?"

"No," Jude admitted. "It wasn't in my view. And even if I'd been able to catch a glimpse as it roared past, it all happened so fast, my mind wasn't on the plate. It was on not hitting the Acura." He winced. "Which I did, anyway."

Blake clapped a hand on his shoulder. "Don't you dare blame yourself for this. That truck was to blame and it sounds like there was nothing you could have done. The car was coming at you."

Jude didn't have time to argue. His attention was drawn to the gurney.

"I see the patient is awake," Blake noted. "I need to see if she's up to answering any questions."

Blake took off, and after a moment's hesitation, Jude followed. Despite their rocky past, despite the way that Ella had cut him out of her life without warning, relief slammed through him when he saw that her beautiful blue eyes were open and that she was talking.

He hadn't seen her in months, but it would be childish of him to walk away.

"How's she doing?" Blake asked Laura. "Is it okay if I ask her a few questions?"

"No broken bones, she's stable." Laura looked at Ella. "Do you feel up to answering the officer's questions?"

"Blake?" Ella squirmed and tried to sit up. A look of misery crossed her face and she rested her head again. Then she saw Jude and her eyes widened. "Jude!"

"Hey, Ella, how are you feeling?" Jude asked, stepping closer so she didn't have to struggle to see him. "That was quite the crash."

She blinked at him. "They said my car rolled."

"It did. You don't remember?" She shook her head, then winced as a whimper slipped through her lips. Despite being awake, she looked to be in rough shape. Clearly in pain.

"Any chance you remember the truck hitting your bumper?" Blake asked. "I got a vague description from Jude, but it would be great if you had more information so we could find the guy."

Her brow furrowed. "I can't recall."

"Is there anything you can tell me?" Blake pressed. "I'd really like to find this guy. What were you doing out this way?"

Her gaze flickered to Jude, as if questioning.

He shrugged.

"I must've been on my way to Jude's," she said. "What else would I be doing on this road?"

"Why?" Blake asked.

Ella's gaze swung to Jude again. "Did we have plans?"

"Why would you have plans?" Blake shot him a skeptical look, then returned his gaze to Ella. "You called off your engagement months ago, and now you're telling me you just casually have plans with Jude?"

"Wh-what?" Ella squirmed again, tried to prop herself into a sitting position, but she groaned and lay back down as the task proved too much of a challenge. "What are you talking about? That's not funny!"

Jude's heart seemed to kick in his chest. He took a step closer, as if Ella's distress was a physical force drawing him in.

"Jude." Ella reached out her hand to him. Then gasped. "My engagement ring. It's gone."

"Right," Blake said, his voice slow and firm, "because you are not engaged."

Ella's eyes widened and she looked frantic as she drew her hand close to her face, as if she needed to study it. As if she thought if she squinted hard enough, the ring would appear. "What? No."

"Just how hard did you hit your head?" Blake muttered.

Laura suddenly looked concerned. "Okay. Enough of this. The last thing we need is for her blood pressure to spike. We need to get her to the hospital for a thorough examination."

"Jude?" Ella's eyes locked on to his. "You'll come, won't you? You'll help me straighten this out?"

He felt Blake's disapproving gaze on him. His friends and family had taken it almost as hard as he had when Ella ended things. But what could he do? Anxiety was buzzing along his spine. Everything about this situation felt wrong. So. Very.

Wrong. Could Ella really not remember? That still didn't explain what she was doing out this way. Presumably, she had to be planning to see him, though he'd been completely unaware. He lived out of town, out in the country, with not a lot of neighbors. Certainly none that Ella knew. There was no other logical explanation for her to be on this road.

Not that visiting him was logical.

"Jude?" She whispered his name, a tearful plea. "Please?"

Colin began to wheel her gurney toward the ambulance.

"Yeah, of course," he called. "I'll meet you at the hospital."

He watched as they loaded her into the back of the ambulance, then closed the doors.

Blake let out a low whistle. "Do you believe that? Do you think she really doesn't remember?"

Jude nodded slowly, his heart banging almost painfully in his chest. "I do."

For one thing, no matter how frustrated he was with her, he knew Ella was not a liar. For another, that was real terror and confusion he had seen on her face.

"Where were you headed?" Blake asked.

Over the last little while, he'd completely forgotten about his sister. She was probably freezing, or at the very least, huddled in front of a space heater, waiting for him. He told Blake as much.

"I can check in on her as soon as I'm done here," Blake offered.

"Hey, guys, look at this," Officer Hernandez said as he approached Blake and Jude. He held a clear plastic bag in his hand, the type that sealed shut with a zipper.

Jude had seen enough evidence bags to realize what it was.

"What did you find?" Blake asked.

"One of the tires on the passenger side blew out—probably what caused the flip. Only, apparently it was shot out. I found this imbedded in the hubcap." He held up the bag, displaying the bullet inside.

Jude's stomach lurched. This was not an accident. Not a case of road rage. Someone had set out to cause Ella harm. No, not just harm. When someone used bullets, they meant business. The realization hit with the force of a physical blow.

The truck hadn't backfired. Someone had fired a gun. There was only one reason someone would do that.

Someone wanted Ella dead.

Ella stared out the hospital window. Under normal circumstances, she'd be enamored with the gorgeous fall foliage on display. A cluster of maple trees sat outside her window. But not now. Today, the crimson and ruby leaves seemed to taunt her.

How could it be October?

It just couldn't be possible.

After being questioned by Dr. Andres, she realized the last memory she had—though it was hazy—was from July. She knew it was July because she recalled being at the black-tie gala fundraiser for the local homeless shelter. With Jude. They'd had such a lovely time at the formal affair. Both dressed up. Him in a tux. Her in an aquamarine dress that matched her eyes. When they'd left, he'd wrapped his jacket around her because the summer air had held a chill.

She shuddered, but not because she was cold.

Her head hurt with a fierceness that she almost couldn't bear. The antinausea meds had kicked in, though. So at least there was that small mercy.

She remembered Jude, of course. Remembered her feelings for him. Yet something felt off. Different. She hadn't sensed that overwhelming sense of love and devotion that she'd felt in the past. Echoes of those feelings lingered, but they were melded with a sense of loss.

And something else.

Unease?

That made no sense.

She had no reason to be uneasy around Jude.

Did she?

A knock on the door yanked her back to the present.

"Come in," she called, fully expecting another nurse to hustle to her side. They had been in multiple times since she'd been brought to a room.

Her breath caught when Jude entered. It hitched again when the doctor who had examined her upon arrival stepped in behind him. The doctor glanced at Jude, then at Ella.

"I have the results of your MRI," Dr. Andres said. "Would you like me to discuss them with you in private?"

"I can leave." Jude stepped back, toward the door that had just whooshed closed.

"Please, stay?" She probably had no right to make the request, yet that didn't stop her from asking—nor did it stop the desperation from creeping into her tone.

Jude hesitated, and her heart dipped. He paused so long that she thought for sure he'd just back out the door without a word.

Instead, he nodded and moved toward her. "Of course."

"The good news," Dr. Andres began, "is that your MRI didn't show any signs of bleeding or swelling in the brain. That rules out the more serious concerns we had when you came in."

That did sound like good news.

"You're experiencing something called post-traumatic retrograde amnesia. It means you've lost memories from before the accident, likely caused by the head trauma." He said the words slowly, as if she might not understand them. Truth be told, on some level, of course, she understood—was expecting a diagnosis such as this even. Yet it didn't make it any easier to wrap her mind around it. Even if it did now have a name.

Post-traumatic retrograde amnesia. She fought back a shudder.

"Retrograde?" Jude asked. He had edged closer to her hospital bed, looking stoic with his arms folded across his chest. His sandy blond hair was rumpled and his pale green eyes had narrowed.

"It means Ella hasn't lost her memory completely, but rather a chunk of time before the accident."

"Right." Jude nodded as if this made sense.

But none of this made sense. Not a single thing made sense from the moment she hazily recalled opening her eyes on that gurney, with the sleet hitting her face and her head pounding as if it housed a herd of wild horses. She pulled in a shaky breath, but even that hurt. The seat belt and air-bag that had teamed up to help save her life had really done a number on her chest and ribs. They ached nearly as badly as her head.

"How long is this going to last? I mean—" Her frantic gaze flickered to Jude, then back to the doctor. "I am going to get my memory back. Aren't I?"

The doctor's expression remained guarded. "Head injuries can be unpredictable. You could regain your memory tomorrow or—"

"Never?" Ella interjected. Her heart began to pound, and suddenly she could feel the blood swishing through her head with every beat. Her vision blurred.

"That is a possibility, but I honestly don't think it's likely."

He gave her a reassuring smile. "Please, don't worry about that now. Stress has never done anyone any good."

Ella blew out a breath, tried to calm herself and nodded. Then she pinched the bridge of her nose and tried to wrangle her thoughts. "I should be grateful I only lost three months. And I am."

It was the truth. But why did they have to be such important months? Missing months where something monumental had happened between herself and Jude. Then again, she had to assume it had been a terrible time. Maybe it was best she'd forgotten what had happened.

"When can I go home?" she asked, embarrassed at how small her voice was, how unsure she sounded.

"Not tonight," Jude blurted, as if he feared that's what she was getting at.

She felt her lower lip begin to tremble, so she clamped it between her teeth. It made sense she that couldn't go home tonight, but she didn't like the thought of being in the hospital, either. Home was where she longed to be—surrounded by her belongings, everything comfortable and familiar.

"Not tonight," the doctor confirmed. "I want to keep you overnight for observation. We'll reassess in the morning. Until then, the best thing you can do for yourself is get some rest. Do you have any questions?"

Yes, she had questions. A million of them.

But none that he could answer.

She knew she probably should ask him more about her condition, but in her muddled state of mind, she couldn't muster anything worth saying.

"No."

"Alright then, try to get a good night's sleep and I'll be back in the morning." With those words, he strode out of the room.

Jude, now looking decidedly uncomfortable, cleared his throat. “So, uh, probably a stupid question, but how are you doing?”

“Not so good.” There was no reason to fib.

“Right.” He tapped his hand against his thigh and his gaze darted toward the window. It wasn’t difficult to sense how agitated he was. Clearly, he wanted to bolt…and she didn’t blame him. “So, um, do you want me to call your parents? Or has someone done that already?”

Her heart stuttered. “My parents. Is my dad okay?”

“Yeah, yeah, he’s fine. No changes,” Jude said assuredly.

Her dad had been diagnosed with Parkinson’s quite some time ago. It had really taken a toll on him…from what she last remembered. Now, months had gone by.

“How do you know?” she demanded.

“He calls to check in with me every once in a while. Has ever since…”

Ever since she’d ended things?

“No, no one has called them. I don’t want you to, either. At least, not tonight. They’ll both just worry. You heard the doctor—stress isn’t good for anyone—and I don’t want to do that to Dad. And Mom, she’s already dealing with enough.” He looked like he was about to argue, so she cut him off. “Not tonight, Jude. Maybe tomorrow.”

Maybe, just maybe, she would have her memory by morning. She sent up a silent prayer.

Jude nodded. “Okay. It’s your call.”

He glanced toward the door, but she needed answers from him before he left.

“What happened? With us? I mean, Blake said I called off the engagement. But I wouldn’t have.” She frowned. “There’s just no way.”

A sharp laugh escaped his lips, and he shook his head. "Oh, darlin', you did."

She realized she was gaping at him in stunned silence when he nodded and said, "It's true."

She shook her head slowly, grateful that there was now only a dull ache. "I wouldn't have," she repeated.

This time, he didn't bother with a response.

After several heartbeats of silence, she realized he was not kidding. She had called off their wedding—had changed the courses of both of their futures. The missing ring only confirmed it.

"Why?" she asked, her tone not hiding her bewilderment.

"Well," he said, "I guess that's a mystery to both of us." He paused, as if deciding what to say. Knowing Jude, he was trying to find a way to be kind, even if she didn't deserve it. "You were acting distant for a few weeks. I knew something was off. I wasn't expecting you to show up at my doorstep one night to hand back my ring. You said you needed to take a break. I was completely blindsided. It's not as if we were two high schoolers trying to decide if our crush was going to last. We're adults—devoted to each other, completely in love. Or so I thought."

She had thought so, too.

Apparently, until she hadn't.

She frowned, trying to make sense of his words. "So I didn't call off the engagement. I just wanted some time. A—a break."

"Ella." He shook his head, his tone emanating hurt and disappointment. "You gave back the ring. You didn't call me again, and you didn't respond when I called you. Weeks went by, and you made it pretty clear that a break really meant a breakup."

How could that be true?

"I must've had a reason," she muttered, more to herself than to him as she tried in vain to remember.

"Yeah," he said, his tone full of hurt. He was gazing at a spot over her head, as if he couldn't bear to look at her. "I'm sure you did. When you remember what that reason was, I'd appreciate it if you let me know. Get some rest, Ella—doctor's orders."

He pivoted and let himself out of her room. No "see you later" or "I'll be back tomorrow." Certainly not an "I love you."

Because he didn't love her anymore. Why would he? And if she was honest with herself, she wasn't entirely sure how she felt about him. Something felt...off.

One more thing she didn't quite understand.

One more thing she didn't have an answer to.

TWO

Jude stepped out into the hallway and blew out a frustrated breath. He forced himself to gather his composure when he realized Blake was striding toward him.

"You okay?" Blake eyed him up, as if he knew the answer. "It's okay to not be okay right now. You've been through a lot tonight. The accident, saving Ella's life by getting her out of a burning car. It had to be a blow to see her after all this time."

"Don't forget the amnesia," Jude muttered.

"Amnesia?" Blake let out a low whistle. "Are you serious?"

"Unfortunately."

"I knew her memory was fuzzy back at the crash site, but I figured she was just woozy. I guess that'll make questioning her difficult."

"It would be pointless," Jude said, just in case his friend decided to give it a go, anyway.

Blake frowned as he glanced at the closed door to Ella's room. "This has been quite an evening."

Jude nodded as his gaze scanned the hallway. He wasn't sure what he was looking for. Trouble, he supposed, or perhaps someone who didn't belong.

Ella was in the hospital, a gash on her head, her memory gone, and though she didn't say it out loud, he could clearly tell she was scared out of her wits. Still, he knew the outcome could've been so much worse.

Someone had blown out her tire. On purpose. Had they actually meant to shoot *her*?

Thank You, God, for protecting her.

He could only imagine how frightening losing one's memory had to be. A chunk of time, months of time, just gone.

"I think I'm going to stay here tonight." The words were out of his mouth before he thought them through. He glanced down the hallway again, first one way, then the other. Nothing seemed amiss. He hadn't spent a lot of time in hospitals, but the hustle and bustle of staff didn't seem out of the ordinary to him. Nor did the concerned visitors walking in and out of rooms down the long hallway.

When he turned to Blake, his friend was staring at him with raised eyebrows.

"I don't want to hear it," Jude muttered.

"I didn't say anything. But since you mentioned it—" Blake gave him a wry grin "—I'm not surprised you would want to stay. What happened was pretty traumatic. Not just for Ella, but for you as well."

"You don't think it makes me pathetic? Considering how things ended with us?"

"Pathetic?" Blake shook his head. "Nah. I think it just speaks to your character. You're a good guy and always do the right thing. You're the guy everyone counts on when things start to fall apart."

Jude wasn't sure about that, but he appreciated the sentiment.

"I did talk to hospital security," Blake said. "They are aware of the situation. I asked them to keep an eye on Ella's room. They're short-staffed—who isn't these days—but they did say they'd double up on their rounds of this floor. That bullet puts a whole different spin on things. What happened out on that road, it wasn't just an accident."

"I'm glad you let Security know," Jude said. He was relieved that the nurses' station wasn't far away, either. The more eyes on Ella's room, the better.

"I stopped by Lexie's, let her know what was up," Blake said. "She told me to tell you not to worry about her, she'll figure something out."

Jude felt a niggle of guilt. He hated to bail on his sister. Yet, he knew she would be okay. He couldn't say the same about Ella. What if she never got her memory back?

Blake glanced at his watch. "I've still got a few hours left of my shift. Since I can't question Ella, I had better get back out there. Give me a call if you need anything."

"Will do," Jude said, grateful for the support.

Blake strode away, and Jude turned back to Ella's room. He couldn't get himself to leave. But he wasn't in the mental frame of mind to go back inside, either. He needed to tell Ella, or someone did, that her tire had been shot out. Yet, maybe that could wait until morning. She needed rest, and the doctor had instructed her to relax, and knowing someone had tried to kill her would obviously do the opposite. The truth could wait one more day.

Seeing her tonight, pulling her unconscious body from the car, had elicited a myriad of turbulent emotions. He had spent months getting over her, but he'd never wanted to see her harmed, and he was so grateful she was okay.

His stomach growled ferociously, reminding him that hours had passed since this ordeal had started. Normally, he'd have eaten dinner long before now. Pushing off from the wall, he decided to head to the cafeteria. It should still be open a bit longer. Maybe once his stomach was full, he'd be able to think more clearly, make a plan—something that went beyond just hanging out at the hospital like some lurker.

He stopped at the nurses' station and asked the receptionist to keep an eye on Ella's room and he let her know he'd be back shortly.

Fifteen minutes later, after waiting in line for a roast-beef sandwich, an apple and a large coffee, he headed back upstairs. He finished off the sandwich in the time it took him to climb the stairwell. He needed to talk to Ella, let her know he planned on staying. His hope was that it would ease some of her worry because he hated seeing that look of fear in her eyes.

He knew that if *he* was hospitalized, he'd want someone there for moral support.

So that's what he'd do—be there for moral support. He'd be a friend. He'd ask the hospital staff for a chair and sit outside of her door. Under the circumstances, he could put their hurtful past behind him. It had been months. It was time to move on.

Friends.

The word reverberated around in his brain. Sure. They could be friends. It would be better than the silence that had settled between them since she'd walked away.

He dodged a harried teen who was looking at her phone instead of where she was going. After a near collision and a hasty apology from the girl, he glanced down the hallway toward Ella's room again. A flurry of movement caught his eye.

Someone slipped into her room. Not a nurse. Not a doctor. A man in jeans and a burgundy hoodie, the hood pulled low to shadow his face. Jude's gut clenched because the scenario felt all wrong to him.

Who wore a hood indoors? More importantly, who, other than law enforcement and Lexie, knew Ella was here?

He tossed the rest of his unfinished apple and coffee into the garbage can as he rushed down the hallway. His boots hammered against the tile as he closed the distance in long, panicked strides.

His heartbeat thundered in his ears. Every instinct screamed that something was wrong.

He flung the door open to find the man standing over Ella.

She was thrashing.

It took Jude only an instant to realize the man was holding a pillow over her head.

"Stop!" Jude roared as he lunged into the room. Then he yelled over his shoulder, "Call Security!"

He didn't wait for a response.

The moment of distraction cost him. When he whipped his head back around, he was met with a fist to the face. Pain cracked through his jaw and stars exploded behind his eyes.

He staggered backward as the man charged past him. Jude hit the wall, then bounced forward and rushed to the door, ready to pursue.

Ella's weak, gasping moan stopped him.

He whirled back to the bed, his heart racing as tears streamed down Ella's ashen face.

The pillow was lying in a harmless heap on the floor.

"Get Security! That man tried to kill this patient!" he shouted into the hallway, relieved when he saw a nurse already on the phone, wide-eyed and nodding at him to let him know she understood.

He was torn—wanting to race after the assailant, but needing to be sure Ella was okay.

"Get me out of here!" she cried as she struggled to sit, then swung her legs over the bed.

"No, you should have a doctor check you over." He couldn't leave with her. Could he?

She shook her head. "I thought the rollover was an accident."

Jude hadn't told her about the bullet. She seemed so fragile, it didn't seem like the right time.

"But now this? Someone is trying to kill me." She slid from the bed and wobbled on her feet. "I won't stay here. I don't feel safe here."

Jude could not argue.

Instead, he scooped her into his arms as she took a stumbling step forward. She shivered violently and that sealed his decision. The hallway was bustling with activity as nurses discussed what had just happened. He didn't see a security guard yet, and he wasn't about to wait around for one. He heard one of the nurses shout after him as he rushed down the hallway.

He ignored her. He had one thing on his mind. He needed to get Ella out of the hospital.

Now.

Ella clung to Jude as he refused to release her. He hustled down the hallway

She had asked him to put her down, but he either didn't hear her, or he was ignoring her. Truth be told, she wasn't sure she could move as quickly as she would have liked, so maybe it was for the best. She squeezed her eyes shut as she tried to ignore the pain ricocheting through her head.

She was only vaguely aware of a door opening, then Jude trotting down the stairs with her still in his arms. It seemed like an interminable amount of time, and then she felt the brisk autumn breeze blow against her face.

With effort, she peeled her eyes open. They were in the parking lot. Drizzle was falling from the sky.

"I'm getting you out of here," Jude murmured, his voice low and comforting next to her ear.

He hurriedly crossed the lot, heading toward his truck.

He jostled her a bit and she realized he was searching for his keys as he moved. Using the fob, he clicked the lock, then tugged the door open. He gently hoisted her up and into the seat, settling her inside.

Then he jogged around to the driver's door and let himself in.

Something caught her eye near her feet. She leaned over, ever so slowly, and tugged up her purse. Jude opened the driver's door and hopped inside. He glanced at her lap.

"Oh, I grabbed that out of your car at the crash site. I figured you would want it kept safe. I didn't think to bring it into the hospital."

"Thank you for doing that." She hugged it to her chest, feeling a sense of security from the only bit of normalcy all evening. Funny how she hadn't even thought about asking for her purse, or subsequently her phone and wallet. Clearly, her mental acuity was not up to par.

He looked at her with uncertainty, and maybe a hint of guilt, flickering across his face.

"I don't know what to do," he admitted.

"Get us out of here?" she offered.

"You're hurt. You've been admitted to the hospital. Your doctor said he wants to keep you overnight, keep you for observation." He hesitated. "It feels wrong, just leaving with you. I can't just take you away from here."

"Can't you?" she wondered. "I might not be thinking clearly, but it's pretty obvious someone has tried to kill me twice in a matter of hours." She shuddered, cold dread spilling down her spine, pooling in her stomach, making her ill. A tremor racked her body, the weight of the evening pressing down harder than ever. “The doctor also said the best thing for me is to rest, recuperate and to not stress. If I go back in there, I’m going to feel like I’m lying in bed with a target on my forehead.” She gathered her resolve. “Actually, I’m not going back in. I’m not a prisoner. No one can make me stay here. If you won’t get me out of here, I’ll find another way.”

“Alright,” Jude said and started the truck. But he didn’t back out. “I don’t know where to take you. Your parents’? That would get you out of town.” They lived several hours away, in Helena where Ella had grown up.

“No. I already told you how I feel about worrying them right now. Mom has her hands full caring for Dad. I don’t want her to feel obligated to take care of me, too.”

So where was she going to go?

A friend? Which friend was she willing to put at risk?

A hotel?

“You can take me home. Or maybe my antique shop would be better.” Her store, Ella’s Attic, had a back room she could crash in. It had a passably comfy couch and she had a small kitchenette. She even kept a change of clothes in a small closet in case she spilled a cup of tea on her lap. Though she’d only done that once, it was enough to make her want to be prepared.

But would her attacker find her there?

“I don’t think that’s a good idea,” Jude said. “Both places are too obvious. If this guy came into a hospital, where there are hundreds of people, what’s to stop him from barging into your house or shop?”

The thought of being tracked down sent shivers shimmying down her spine.

He was right and she knew it. No point in protesting.

Ella leaned back against the headrest. She was exhausted, every part of her body felt heavy, and she was weary to the bone. She had only meant to put her head back, maybe rest her eyes while she mulled over the problem and tried to come up with a solution.

But the next thing she knew, Jude's truck was bumping down a rutted driveway. She sat up, fought down a groan of pain and squinted as she took in her surroundings.

They were at Jude's ranch—one of her favorite places in all the world, and now, more than ever, it looked like a safe haven, a sanctuary. The house came into view first, a two-story log home with a wide, wraparound porch, its cedar beams weathered to a warm honey-gold. A wrought-iron table and chairs sat on one side, with two rocking chairs on the other.

Beyond the house stood the big red barn, its paint slightly faded but it was still a proud structure, flanked by a corral and split-rail fences that stretched toward the foothills. A sprawling pasture, edged with golden grass and scrub pines, held the gentle movement of horses—his rescues.

While Jude worked full-time as a game warden, he was also a quiet savior of animals most people overlooked. He had a habit of attending auctions and buying the horses no one else wanted—the old, the sick, the forgotten. Instead of being funneled through the auction pipeline to who knew where, they came here. To *him.* To this place, where they could live out their years with dignity, full bellies and grass beneath their hooves.

She could just make out the silhouettes of two of her favorite girls, Clementine and Ramona, standing side by side near the fence line, their heads low and tails swishing lazily. A little farther off, a trio of elderly geldings grazed contentedly, moving slowly but surely, safe at last.

How could she ever have stopped loving this big-hearted

man, who had turned what was once a simple hobby farm into a rescue ranch of grace and redemption?

"You brought me to your place?" Ella's voice came out scratchy and hoarse. The nap she'd taken hadn't helped. If anything, she felt heavier. Like she could sleep for a hundred years and still wake up tired.

"I did," Jude said simply.

"Why?"

"There weren't a lot of good options." His tone was calm, measured. "In fact, I couldn't think of a single other option. So here we are."

Her gaze drifted to the window. It was dark and the porch light glowed softly, illuminating a second vehicle in the drive—one she recognized.

Her stomach sank.

There was movement at the front door.

Lexie.

The porch light silhouetted her small frame. Arms folded. Still as a statue. Watching.

Ella didn't say anything, but Jude let out a low breath like he hadn't expected to see his sister there, either.

"Wait here." He climbed out of the truck without a word and strode toward the house.

They spoke briefly—too far away for Ella to hear the exchange—but the tension in Jude's posture was clear. His shoulders were tight. His hands moved as he spoke, while Lexie barely budged. Her arms stayed crossed the whole time, and when she finally stepped aside, it was with the stiff, reluctant grace of someone tolerating a decision she didn't agree with.

Ella swallowed hard, suddenly wishing she was invisible. She and Lexie had been close at one time. But Lexie and Jude were close as well, and it seemed that if Lexie had to choose sides in the breakup that Ella didn't remember, Lexie was choosing her brother's side.

Of course, it only made sense that she would.

Jude returned and opened her door. His expression had settled back into neutral, but she could tell that Lexie being here had rattled him.

"Let me guess," she said quietly. "Lexie hates me."

"She doesn't hate you." His jaw flexed. "She's just…protective."

Protective. That was one way to put it. Ella didn't blame her. Lexie had always been fiercely loyal. And Ella had disappeared without a word. Had apparently broken Jude's heart and walked away.

She looked down at herself—bare feet, hospital gown. She was a mess. Fighting down a whimper, she started to ease herself out of the truck.

He arched an eyebrow. "You're barefoot."

"I'll be fine."

"The ground's probably freezing. It's been sleeting on and off."

Still, she hesitated. It felt like all she had left was her dignity, and even that was hanging by a thread.

"I'll carry you," he said, softer this time, his voice almost a plea that dug at her heart. "Please."

She gave in with a nod, biting her lip as he lifted her gently and shut the truck door with his hip. The moment he stepped onto the porch, Lexie's voice cut through the stillness like a blade.

"How gallant."

Ella winced. She didn't have to look at Lexie to feel the judgment in her tone. It clung to her skin like cold mist.

"She's barefoot, okay?" Jude grumbled. "Ease up."

He didn't slow as they stepped past his sister and into the

house. The air inside was warm, but Ella still felt a chill, and it wasn't just from the cold.

Jude settled her gently on the living room couch. She shifted, trying not to look as self-conscious as she felt. She didn't belong here. Not anymore. Not after everything.

Lexie hovered near the doorway, her gaze unreadable, her arms still folded like she was bracing for a fight.

"You're staying here?" Ella asked softly.

Lexie shrugged. "Furnace went out. My house is freezing."

Ella glanced at Jude.

"That's where I was headed before—" he paused, wincing "—well, before your accident. I was going to work on the furnace."

"Blake stopped by to let me know about your accident, then called later telling me what happened in the hospital." She shrugged. "It's cheaper to call a repairman in the morning, during business hours, and I thought the two of you could use the company. I got here right before you did."

Ella didn't have anything to say to that, nor did she think Lexie wanted a reply. Jude must've called Blake with an update while she'd accidentally dozed off. He would've wanted someone—law enforcement—to know what had happened and where she had gone.

"I brought that for you," Lexie motioned toward a pink duffel bag sitting on the coffee table. "I figured you wouldn't have any clothes. I'm a size smaller than you so I just brought some yoga pants and a few of my bigger T-shirts."

It wasn't an insult, it was the truth. Lexie was petite while Ella considered herself average. She was grateful that despite Lexie's annoyance with her, she'd been thoughtful enough to do something so kind.

"Thank you. I'll be happy to get out of this hospital gown," Ella said.

Lexie offered a brief nod, then turned and disappeared down the hallway.

Ella let out a slow breath. "She really doesn't want me here."

"She's looking out for me," Jude said quietly.

Ella nodded, saying nothing. What was there to say?

A familiar *thump* broke the quiet.

Then came the scratchy tap of claws on hardwood and the unmistakable guttural yowl of a cantankerous old cat.

Ella blinked. "Bandit?"

The gray tomcat emerged from the hallway, his gait awkward but determined, the tilt of his head just as she remembered. One eye blinked up at her while the other—which was long gone—was marked by an old, jagged scar. The stump of his tail twitched as he sniffed the air and headed straight for her like a heat-seeking missile.

"Hey, buddy," she whispered, sinking a hand into his thick fur as he hopped up and settled on her lap without hesitation. He purred louder than an outboard motor. The heavy, familiar rumbling sound soothed the edges of her frayed heart.

She couldn't help but smile. At least someone was happy to see her.

Jude, still standing nearby, crossed his arms and shook his head. "Unbelievable. I'm the one who rescued him out of a blizzard with a fractured leg and half a tail. Nearly had my own eyes clawed out as I tried to treat him. And it's you he melts all over."

Ella, to her relief, remembered *that* story. Jude had been out on a snowmobile patrol, checking for registrations, reckless operation, that sort of thing, when he nearly ran over what he thought was a clump of frozen ice on one of the public trails. Until the gray blob lifted its head. Realizing it was a half-frozen cat, he scooped up the emaciated ball of fur and stuffed the feline into his jacket, where he stayed until the end of Jude's shift—no doubt, absorbing every bit of his rescuer's warmth—then brought him home and doctored him up until he could get him into the vet the next day.

Bandit, as if on cue, flipped onto his side and pressed himself even deeper into Ella's lap, full body vibrating with joy.

Ella smiled softly as she ruffled his fur. "Well, he has good taste."

Jude grunted, but there was a flicker of amusement beneath his scowl. "Yeah, well, he's a traitor."

She looked up at him. "He's loyal. Just…selectively."

Jude rolled his eyes, but a faint smirk tugged at the edge of his mouth. It disappeared almost as quickly as it came. What had chased the smile away? Was he thinking that she wasn't loyal?

"Lexie set up the den for you," he said. "The futon isn't the comfiest bed in the house, but she thought it would be better than climbing the stairs with your injuries."

"That was thoughtful of her," Ella said, once again grateful that her old friend had put aside her anger and had shown kindness.

Jude nodded. "Do you need help with anything?"

"No, I can manage," Ella said quietly, shifting Bandit off her lap and standing…slowly, carefully. Her legs still felt like cooked noodles, but she didn't want him to see that. His lips turned downward, as if he was aware of every ache and pain, regardless of her effort to hide it.

"Alright then, I'm going to check in with Blake again. He said he'd be sure someone patrolled the property during the night." He moved toward the kitchen, then looked over his shoulder. "Sleep well."

Before she could reply, he was gone. With a grimace she grabbed the duffel bag and shuffled toward her makeshift bedroom.

Bandit trailed after her like a shadow.

Five minutes later, she was in soft flannel pajamas, curled up beneath the quilt. Bandit had claimed the spot beside her, his body warm against her hip. His purring was gentle and soothing, keeping the room from being too silent.

For a few moments she stared into the darkness, her mind churning and her heart aching. She prayed to regain her memory by morning.

She drifted off, knowing that Jude was down the hall, and while they were no longer together, she had faith that he'd keep her safe through the night.

THREE

Jude glanced at the clock above the kitchen sink, watching the minutes tick by. It was nearly nine. Ella was still sleeping. Years ago, people believed that someone with a concussion shouldn't sleep too long. But he'd had one himself a few years back, when a novice canoer had asked for help loading their canoe onto the roof of their SUV. The teen had lost his grip and it crashed down on Jude's head, hard enough to knock him off balance and leave him with a mild concussion. He knew now that the old thinking had changed. Rest wasn't dangerous. It was essential for the brain to heal.

Another glance at the clock had him feeling impatient. He knew Ella was a morning person. Would it be appropriate for him to go check on her? Lexie had left to meet a repairman an hour ago. Now, she was probably at work, where she served as a front-desk supervisor at a local hotel.

He'd already gone out to give his geriatric herd fresh water and their special senior feed.

The soft click of a door down the hallway had him pushing away from the countertop. He started to cross the kitchen to check on Ella. Then he stopped himself. There was no need to act like an overprotective…what? Friend?

He didn't need to hover. Lexie had told him as much before she left this morning. Or perhaps "lectured him profusely on the matter" would be a more apt description of the conversation.

He moved back to the window and glanced outside, not really paying attention to the view of the sprawling ranch, the familiar pasture dotted with horses. It was a distraction, though a poor one. The moment he heard Ella's padded footfalls enter the kitchen, he whirled to face her.

Real smooth, he chastised himself.

She looked…well, terrible. Terrible in a way that twisted his heart and made his soul ache. Though he knew better than to say it out loud. She had dark circles under her eyes, her footsteps were slow and deliberate and she seemed to be wincing in pain. Her ebony curls were in a wild tangle around her head. She had on a pair of black yoga pants and a bright pink T-shirt that he'd seen Lexie wear a handful of times.

He reached toward the bottle of ibuprofen his sister had left on the countertop. "Lexie said you may want to take one of these when you get up. How are you doing?"

It seemed like a ridiculous question. How did he think she was doing? But what else was he supposed to say?

"Better," she said, shuffling toward him.

He couldn't help but arch a suspicious eyebrow at her.

"I said better, not fantastic." She dropped down into a chair at the kitchen table. "And that's the truth. One of the nurses told me our bodies want to heal, and they will, if we give them enough time and rest."

That made sense.

He filled a glass of water for her and shook two of the small pills into his palm, then crossed the room and handed them to her.

"Thank you," she said, taking both instantly and confirming his suspicion that she was still hurting.

"Are you hungry?"

"I am," she admitted, almost apologetically.

"I can scramble some eggs," he offered.

"You've already done so much for me. I'm sure you're anxious to get me off your hands."

Was he? He should be, but he wasn't so sure that was the case. He was torn. Being with Ella, at one time, was all he'd ever wanted. Now? Well, best not to let his mind, or his heart, go there.

Instead of addressing her statement, he moved on.

"Breakfast is no problem."

"I'd really appreciate toast. I'm still just a bit queasy and I'm not sure my stomach is up to eating eggs."

"You got it."

While the bread was toasting, he poured two glasses of orange juice. Ella didn't care for coffee and after their breakup, he'd tossed out her favorite box of tea because he had no intention of drinking it. When the toast popped up, Jude buttered the slices, then spread on a thick layer of peanut butter, just how he knew she liked it. Next, he put the glasses and plate on the table before slipping into a chair across from her.

She thanked him and then took a tentative bite. Apparently, her stomach was not going to revolt over the toast and she finished it off, as if she were ravenous. He realized she probably was. While he'd chowed down on a huge serving of leftover chili last night, even after eating in the hospital cafeteria, Ella had gone to bed without dinner.

"Can I get you anything else?"

"This is plenty, thank you."

"Lexie suggested you try to get into your doctor today. I'm sure you don't want to go back to the hospital, but she feels that you really ought to be checked out again." He wanted to ask her if her memory was back, but he felt fairly certain that she would've said so if it had returned.

"I suppose that's not a bad idea," she admitted, now nibbling on the second piece of toast.

"I'll drive you."

She paused, then set the toast on the plate. "Wait. What day is it? Aren't you supposed to be at work?"

"It's Tuesday, and yes, usually. I have the day off."

"Have it off?" She narrowed her eyes at him.

"Fine. I took it off."

"I hate having you waste your vacation time on me."

He didn't bother to tell her that he had plenty of vacation time to waste. Originally, he'd asked for two weeks off for their wedding and honeymoon. They had planned to rent an RV and visit national parks around the West. Obviously, that time-off request had been canceled.

"We have a couple of new hires, both part-timers, that are anxious for more hours. Yolanda and Barry. Both were more than happy to take my shifts through the rest of the week." Entirely true and he knew they'd be ready and willing to step in if he asked for even more time off.

Frown lines furrowed her brow. "I'm sorry. I hate having you go out of your way for me."

He shrugged. What could he say?

His phone rang, saving him from having to say anything. It was resting on the counter. The display showed it was a call from Blake, which really wasn't a surprise.

His friend had touched base last night, letting him know that the security cameras at the hospital hadn't caught anything useful and the assailant had gotten away.

"What's up?" he asked, by way of greeting.

"Is Ella still with you?"

"For now, yes." He glanced at her—she was eating her toast again, chewing slowly and eyeing him curiously.

"I hate being the bearer of more bad news, but her house was broken into in the middle of the night."

Jude's spine stiffened. "How do you know that?"

"We got a call this morning from one of Ella's neighbors. They'd gotten up with their newborn and noticed a light in the house. But not a normal light. Probably a flashlight beam. They thought it was odd, but hadn't heard about Ella's accident yet, so they weren't too suspicious. This morning the gossip mill is churning and they heard about Ella's accident and the attack at the hospital so they called it in." Blake let out a huff of annoyance. "The department had an officer doing drive-bys last night, but they didn't notice anything. It was probably just a matter of timing."

"How do you know the house was broken into? Other than the weird light?" Jude inwardly winced when he saw Ella stiffen, but the question needed to be asked.

"I'm working four ten-hour days so I'm back on duty now. I checked her house out myself. The back door was a bit ajar." Blake hesitated and Jude's stomach dipped in anticipation. "Her house is trashed. Either someone is royally ticked off at her, or they were looking for something. Honestly, I have a hunch it's both. It's a good thing she wasn't there last night, but that goes without saying."

Right. Because would they have tried to kill her again?

Jude didn't know what to say. Sure, he'd been mad at Ella when she'd broken off their engagement. Or more like hurt. But he couldn't imagine anyone else being upset with her. She wasn't the sort of person who just walked around rubbing people the wrong way.

What was going on here?

"Jude? You there?"

"Yeah," he answered, his gaze holding Ella's. "I'm here."

He just didn't know what to say, at least, not with Ella sitting less than ten feet away.

"Okay, it would be great if Ella could come check things out. I understand she's dealing with a concussion, but if she could just look around her place, let us know if anything is missing." Blake paused. "I realize she might not remember enough to know if anything is missing. On the other hand, maybe it could jiggle her memory free."

"Sure," Jude said. "I'll check with her and get back to—"

"What is it?" Ella interjected. "It's pretty clear this conversation has to do with me."

Jude quickly told her about the break-in while Blake waited on the other end of the line.

She stood and pushed back her chair, wincing but looking determined. "Let's go."

"I guess we're leaving now," Jude said to Blake. "We'll see you shortly."

Jude pulled one of his jackets and a pair of flip-flops out of his entryway closet. They weren't ideal, but he was sure Ella wouldn't appreciate him lugging her around his yard again. She slid into them with a muttered thank-you, and an anxious look on her face.

She was quiet on the drive to her house and Jude wasn't sure what to say to her. At one time, he'd known her so well, but now he wasn't sure what was going on in her head. She didn't seem to want to talk and he wasn't going to force it.

Blake met them in Ella's driveway. He warned them of the mess before they entered. Still, his words hadn't prepared either of them for the severity. He had taken pictures and dusted for prints before their arrival, so they were free to go in.

Jude stood back as Ella pressed her hand over her mouth. The chaotic scene at her house was more than a little overwhelming. The place was trashed, with sofa cushions sliced open, broken crystal, drawers overturned, contents of closets and dressers strewn about. The intruder had managed to wreak havoc in her bedroom, home office and living room. A bathroom had been spared, but the kitchen was a disaster. He had tossed a container of milk, a jar of pickles, barbecue sauce and some eggs. The room reeked. Jude couldn't see any reason for the destruction other than the intruder intentionally trying to be destructive. Perhaps he hadn't found what he was looking for so he'd thrown a fit, pitching food and making a mess in an act of rage.

In the past, Jude would've gathered her in his arms, offered words of comfort, murmured that everything would be okay. He would've assured her that they'd get through this.

Together.

Not anymore. Now, the best he could do was offer to help clean up the mess.

"Why would someone do this?" she moaned.

"I was hoping you could tell me."

They both spun around to find a woman standing on the other side of the screen door. They had left the entry door open—as well as opened some windows—in an effort to curtail the growing stench.

"Detective Chen," Jude said, "come on in."

He knew the detective, though not well. Seeing her stirred old, painful memories. His father had been murdered, shot in cold blood, over a decade ago. Detective Chen had been assigned to the case.

A case that was still unsolved and left Jude feeling bitter.

Now was not the appropriate time to take out those feelings so he stuffed them back into the recesses of his mind. He glanced at Blake, who knew his history with the detective, and his friend gave a subtle shrug.

"I can take this from here," the detective told Blake.

For just a moment, Jude thought Blake would protest. But the detective was his superior so he just nodded.

She arched an eyebrow at him. "That means you don't need to stick around. I've got it handled."

Blake's jaw hardened at the blatant dismissal. He headed toward the door. "I'll catch up with you later," he said to Jude.

Once the door clicked shut behind him, the detective turned her attention to Ella. She held out her hand. "I'm Detective Chen. I'll be taking over the investigation."

"Nice to meet you." Ella shook the woman's hand, but her tone wasn't as welcoming as it usually was. Jude suspected she hadn't appreciated Blake's dismissal, either.

"I've been told you have amnesia," Detective Chen said, "but are you up to answering a few questions?"

"Of course." Ella glanced around the living room, then motioned toward the back of the house. She led them, stepping over and around debris, to the sliding glass door off the back of the kitchen. The wicker lounge set on the deck was one of the few things that had not been destroyed. "We'll have to talk back here. It's a bit chilly out."

At least they all still had their coats on.

"This is fine," the detective agreed. "Considering the condition of your house, it seems that the assailant was looking for something. Any idea what that might be?"

Ella hesitated, then shook her head. "No."

"Is there anything missing?"

"Not that I can tell," Ella said. "I have several pieces of vintage Baccarat crystal. It's shattered on the floor of my living room. I don't think any of it was stolen. I also had several antique jewelry pieces that are of considerable value, but they're dumped out on my bedroom floor."

"So it would appear that the intruder wasn't looking for items of value," the detective pointed out.

"I suppose not," Ella said. "Unless they weren't aware how much those pieces were worth. Not everyone is acquainted with the value of such antiquities. But antiques are my passion, my livelihood. It's my business to know."

Detective Chen scribbled a few lines into her notebook before leveling her gaze on Ella again.

"If they weren't searching for something of monetary value, what do you suppose they were searching for?"

Ella's brow furrowed. She glanced at Jude, as if hoping he could help her summon the answer. He gave a subtle shrug.

"I—I don't know," Ella stammered. "I really don't. As you know, I can't remember the last few months. If there's something missing, it's something that I only recently brought home. It's possible there was a valuable find that I brought home. I do that sometimes, for safekeeping. Or if I want to do more research on an item."

"What could they be looking for that's worth killing someone over?" Jude added, his tone hard.

"Exactly what I'd like to know," the detective agreed.

"Do you have any suspects?" he demanded.

She hesitated and Jude thought he saw a flicker of indecision flash across her face. It was gone almost instantly, replaced by carefully schooled features.

"It's too soon to tell." She directed her attention to Ella again.

He didn't like to entertain the idea that he was holding a grudge, but he'd always wondered if a different detective would've solved his father's murder. Landon Sheridan had gone to work, just as he had every day in the eleven years he'd been a game warden. Only, one September evening, he hadn't come home. Jude's mother hadn't been terribly concerned at first, assuming he'd been held up. But as the hours had ticked by, just as worry had started to niggle at her, Landon's supervisor had shown up at their door. He'd held his hat in his hands and had worn the grimmest look Jude had ever seen. Landon had been murdered, shot at the remote location of the Pinecrest Landing, and left there likely midway through his shift.

Haven Creek was a small town, with only one detective in the department. Chen was it. She'd been new, green, and his father's murder had been her first big case. As far as he was concerned, she'd flubbed the investigation. Big-time.

"Hopefully your methods of investigation have improved over the years." He regretted the words the moment he spoke them. They were spiteful, said out of an old hurt, but he couldn't take them back.

She blinked at him, and clenched her jaw as she seemed to take a moment to compose herself.

Guilt needled at him. Maybe he was being unfair. His father's murder scene had been severely compromised, leaving little evidence. It was the primary reason the department had given his family for being unable to solve his murder.

"I assure you, Jude," she began, holding his gaze steady in hers as she made it clear she understood his implication, "that aside from your family, no one wants your father's case solved more than I do."

Hopefully, you do a better job at finding the person after Ella, than you did at finding who killed my father, he thought.

She gave him another moment of her attention, waiting to see if he had another retort. When he said nothing, she seemed to relax slightly.

He leaned back in his chair, allowing himself to observe.

The inquiry seemed pretty standard to Jude, though the detective seemed a bit skeptical over the memory loss. She lobbed questions at Ella, then variations of the same questions, as if trying to trip her up. A common practice with a suspect. But Ella was the victim here.

Wasn't she?

Finally, Detective Chen sliced her gaze to him. "I'd like to speak with Ella alone for a few moments." Her tone was polite, yet held a command. "Would you mind giving us some privacy?"

Ella cast a resigned look his way. He knew she was worn-out, both physically and emotionally. He wanted to tell the detective no, that he would prefer to stay. Ella looked as if she needed the support. Detective Chen looked determined to see her demand met.

He reminded himself Ella wasn't his responsibility and complied with the detective's request. He headed back inside, went to the kitchen, dug around in the pantry for a garbage bag and began to clean up the worst of the mess.

He dropped a cracked dish into the garbage bag and paused, listening to the faint murmur of voices on the porch. Was he wrong to leave her out there alone? Or worse…was he wrong to trust that Ella was the victim here? Something about Chen's questioning wasn't adding up, and he hated that he wasn't sure who, or what to believe when the stakes were so high.

Ella knew Detective Chen was on her side, knew she wanted this case solved. She wasn't sure why, then, the detective's scrutinizing gaze made her feel so uncomfortable. She shifted in her chair, folded her hands on the table and waited for the questioning to resume.

"I've found that sometimes people are more comfortable, more open, when they're questioned alone," she began.

"There's nothing I can tell you that I wouldn't say in front of Jude," Ella said.

"Are you sure about that?"

"Yes." She was sure, wasn't she? Why, suddenly, did the detective's question make her doubt herself? Or…doubt Jude? No. That was absurd. Though why, then, had she broken off their engagement? What had happened? It had to have been something monumental because from every memory she could recall, Jude meant the world to her. Doubts churned inside her—baseless, yet persistent, because never had something made less sense to her.

She blinked back at the detective. Now was not the time to let her mind meander down memory lane.

The detective studied her and Ella fought the urge to squirm.

"Officer Thompson mentioned you stayed at Jude's last night. He was at the hospital with you, and also at the crash site. Are the two of you close?"

Ella shifted uncomfortably. "He's my ex-fiancé."

"I see. Is there anything else you'd like to share with me?" Detective Chen leaned forward, her gaze locking with Ella's. Her tone was firm, yet sincere, when she said, "You can trust me, Ella. You can tell me anything. You know I'm here to help."

Ella frowned. It seemed to her as if there was a hidden meaning in the detective's words, her tone and expression. Something she should understand, but couldn't quite decipher. She sucked in a little gasp. No. Oh, no.

"Hold up a minute," she said. "You don't think Jude has something to do with this, do you? Is that why you asked him to leave?" Her gaze darted toward the house and she lowered her voice. "That couldn't be possible. He was in another vehicle. He'd never hurt me. And he was at the ranch all night. There's no way he could've trashed my house."

At least, she thought he was at the ranch all night, but she'd slept straight through.

He certainly wasn't the one who attempted to suffocate her in the hospital. But did the detective think he was tied to it all somehow?

"No," Detective Chen said, leaning back in her chair again, looking decidedly disappointed. "I don't think he had anything to do with your accident. Or trashing your house."

Confusion slid through Ella's mind. Were her thoughts still muddled? Or was there something else going on here? Why did it seem as if the detective expected her to read between the lines? She mentally shook away the thought. She was being ridiculous. Having such a gaping hole in her memory was really messing with her head.

But still, she couldn't help but wonder.

"Am I missing something?" She scoffed, embarrassed at her word choice. "I mean, something other than the past several months?"

The detective cast a grim smile her way, but didn't answer her question. Instead, she handed her a card with her information on it. She took Ella by surprise when she clasped her hand in her own.

Ella looked up, meeting the detective's intense gaze. The woman's dark eyes seemed to dig into her, as if trying to dig into her soul. Or her memory? The intensity was almost disconcerting. Something else *was* going on here. Ella was sure of it. But what?

"If you remember, remember anything at all," Detective Chen stated, "don't hesitate to give me a call. Day or night. You know we both want the same thing here. Justice."

Ella nodded, feeling numb and more confused than ever. *Did* she know they wanted the same thing? Was that a generic statement? Or was there a deeper meaning?

Was she overthinking this?

Oh, God, please let me get my memory back. I feel like I'm completely losing my mind here.

"Are you going to be staying at the ranch for a while?" Detective Chen asked.

"I—I think maybe that's the plan. Though Jude didn't really confirm that yet. I hate to be a burden, so I could stay at my shop." She glanced toward the door. "I don't feel comfortable staying here, at my house. Not after seeing what they did to the place. At least my shop has a top-notch security system."

"It's also closer to the police station," the detective pointed out. "If you do decide to stay there, be sure to let me know. I'll ensure that someone from the department keeps an eye on the place."

Ella nodded, but a small shiver ran down her spine. Maybe it was just the chill in the air. Or maybe it was something in the detective's tone—something she couldn't quite put her finger on.

She brushed aside the feeling. She had bigger things to worry about than second-guessing the people trying to protect her.

The detective slid her chair back. "I'll see myself out. And don't worry, I'll be in touch."

She watched as Detective Chen walked around the house without giving her a backward glance. A few moments later, she heard a car engine fire up, then Jude came out the back door.

He wore a quizzical look. "How did that go?"

Ella rubbed her temple. "I honestly don't know. I've never been questioned by the police before. It was…intense."

"That's pretty typical," he said.

Was it? She supposed so.

"I didn't realize that Detective Chen was who worked

on your father's case," she said softly. He had talked about his father's death, but not at length, and Ella had imagined after all this time it was still too painful. She knew he was disappointed in the local department, but as far as she could remember, he'd never named anyone specific. Ella hadn't grown up here, so hadn't been around at the time. She'd only come to Haven Creek six years ago, when she'd run across an ad for an antique shop for sale.

Jude's expression clouded over and it was clear seeing Chen again had brought old hurts to the surface.

"Yes, she was the detective on the case. She'd been with the department less than a year." He dragged a hand through his hair. "Listen, I know I shouldn't have called her out like that. It wasn't appropriate. Quite frankly, I'd rather not discuss my dad right now. We have more important things to deal with. Like getting you in for a checkup with your doctor."

"Sure. Of course." Ella's heart twisted. There was a time when Jude would have opened up to her, would've wanted to talk about how seeing Detective Chen had affected him. But not now, not when they were on such shaky emotional ground with one another. He could blame it on her medical condition, but she knew he was simply shutting her out. Considering her circumstances, that shouldn't hurt. But it did.

She frowned.

Maybe that was it. Maybe the friction between Detective Chen and Jude was what had caused the detective's odd behavior. It was possible he had rattled her with his abrasive insult. But if that was the case, if the detective had an issue with Jude...why did Ella feel as if the woman thought *she* was hiding something?

FOUR

Jude coasted to a stop at the end of Ella's block as he waited for her to end her phone call.

"Thank you for squeezing me in," she said, then disconnected. With a sigh, she slid her phone into her purse. "I can't get in to see Dr. Ingalls for another two hours. She's booked solid but is willing to squeeze me in around her lunch break, which I feel guilty about, but her nurse was insistent, especially after hearing about the…ordeal last night."

He eased his foot off the brake. Traffic was minimal, and no one looked suspicious.

"Back to the ranch then, for an hour or so?"

Ella's phone rang again and Jude's gut clenched. Something about the sharp sound of her ringtone made every instinct in him jolt to high alert.

"Oh, maybe that's the doctor's office calling me back," she mused. "They said they would if they had a cancellation."

Jude continued slowly down the road. He'd just turned toward the ranch, but if Ella's doctor could get her in sooner, they'd have to turn back around.

"Hello?" Ella paused briefly, then said with surprise, "Oh! Detective Chen. I wasn't expecting to hear from you so soon."

Jude darted a glance her way. She met his eyes with a furrowed brow and a shrug.

"Yes, I think we can do that. We can be there in ten minutes. Does that work for you?"

Jude pulled over to the shoulder as Ella ended her call. "What was that about?"

"She asked if we could meet her at my antique shop."

"Why?"

"She said she hoped something there would jolt my memory."

Jude shrugged as he turned his truck around. "I guess it wouldn't hurt, if you feel up to it."

He glanced at her. She did not look up to it, but she nodded regardless. The shadows under her eyes had darkened, and she wore a slight grimace.

"We don't have to do this," he said. "The detective can wait."

"It's okay," Ella said. "I don't know if *I* can wait. If there's a chance that something—anything—will help me remember, I need to look into it."

She glanced at the dashboard clock. "Besides, if we went back to the ranch, it wouldn't be long before we'd have to turn around and come back to town for my appointment. Might as well make use of our time."

Jude's hand tightened on the steering wheel. Seeing her push forward like this—battered, scared, but stubbornly determined—hit something raw inside him. She wasn't giving up. She never had. It reminded him of those first few years when she'd opened Ella's Attic, the economy had been rough. But she'd remained optimistic and had persevered.

A small voice inside him warned that someone else wasn't giving up, either—the person trying to take her out for good.

They drove back to town in silence, mostly because Ella had rested her head on the back of the seat and closed her eyes. Jude didn't think she was sleeping, but he was glad that she was at least resting. Her eyes fluttered open when he pulled into a parking spot right in front of the building.

She glanced around.

"I don't see Detective Chen's vehicle yet," he said. "Do you want to wait for her, or should we go in?"

"Let's go in," Ella said with a sigh. "It might be helpful for me to look around."

When they entered Ella's Attic, they were greeted by the familiar scents of dried apples and cinnamon potpourri.

Ella left the sign flipped to Closed, but didn't lock the door.

"Detective Chen should be here any minute." She glanced around before turning to Jude. "Do you mind if I just wander?"

"Have at it," he replied.

The shelves were lined with an abundance of treasures. He watched as Ella wandered down the center aisle of her store. Every few feet she stopped to pick up an item and inspect it, making him think it was something "new," or at least something she had acquired in the last few months.

He remained quiet, hoping that if he gave her space, it would help free up her memories.

But he couldn't help trailing behind her, every protective instinct in him keyed up.

As they crossed to her office, Jude's eyes caught movement outside the back window. A shadow? A flicker of something pulling back into the alley? He stiffened but said nothing, wanting to be sure before sounding the alarm. Maybe it was nothing. Maybe it was everything.

The back window faced the alley and allowed only minimal sunlight to come in.

He was half expecting to find the room trashed, but it was as neat as always. The room held a puffy couch, a coffee table, a small fridge and a toaster oven. She often stayed at the shop all day rather than take a lunch break, so the room was well equipped.

Ella let out a little growl of frustration as she entered her personal space and looked around.

"It was silly of me to hope that just being in a familiar place would make my memory come rushing back."

She gasped when the window behind her shattered. Glass sprayed into the room. It took Jude only a split second to ascertain the cause.

"Pipe bomb!" he shouted, grabbing her by the arm and nearly yanking her off her feet.

He shoved Ella in front of him as they ran through the shop, toward the front door.

Please, God. Please, God. The simple plea played on a silent loop in Jude's mind as they raced toward safety. He trusted that the Lord knew exactly what he was asking, even if his mind couldn't finish forming a coherent prayer.

They reached the door and opened it, had barely touched the sidewalk when the bomb exploded.

A deafening sound filled the air. The building shook as Jude dove toward the sidewalk with Ella in his arms. He landed hard on his side, managing to take the brunt of their impact, as he twisted his body so she landed on top of him. Even in his hastened state, he was aware of trying to protect her head.

People on the street screamed and ran. Others, who'd been inside, poked their heads out to look for the source of the noise.

Jude took a moment to catch his breath, to assess himself for injuries even as he asked Ella, "Are you okay?"

"I think so," she said, her tone breathless.

They slowly sat up, coughing through the haze of dust and debris that hung heavy in the air.

Detective Chen came sprinting down the sidewalk toward them, her badge flashing at her hip, one hand resting on the weapon in her holster.

"Are you alright?" she cried, skidding to a stop beside them, her eyes scanning Ella from head to toe.

"Yeah," Jude said hoarsely as he lurched to his feet. He reached down and gently pulled up Ella beside him, his arm steadying her trembling form. "I think we're okay. Definitely a bit rattled."

Ella stared at the front of her shop, her chest heaving, her lips parted in disbelief. Her eyes shimmered with unshed tears, but she blinked rapidly, trying to stay composed.

From the outside, the building looked intact—no scorched walls, no visible flame—but Jude knew better. He'd seen the dividing wall begin to crumble, felt the intensity of the blast chase them through the store like a monstrous wave.

The interior would be damaged by smoke, the merchandise ruined, her dreams blackened by ash and broken glass.

"I've called for backup," Chen said, turning a slow circle to monitor the rapidly growing crowd. Sirens echoed from nearby streets, and would soon be converging on their location.

"We need to get off the sidewalk. Whoever did this might still be watching."

Jude's gaze swept the street, instinctively searching for threats.

A man stood half-hidden in the mouth of the alley across the street—hands stuffed into his pockets, his posture too stiff, too alert. As soon as Jude locked eyes with him, the man pivoted sharply and melted into the crowd.

Just a gawker? Or the culprit? He was already gone as Jude took a staggering step, his ears still ringing from the blast.

Too many faces. Too many onlookers with phones in hand, wide eyes and gaping mouths. But any one of them could be the person who'd tried to kill Ella.

"I'd like you to meet me at the station," Chen added, her tone tight with urgency. She lowered her voice. "But first, let's move. Now."

Ella gave a stiff nod, but her legs faltered. Jude caught her around the waist, holding her upright.

"Let's go," he whispered.

They pushed through the gathering crowd, Chen nudging them forward. Jude's eyes darted to every face, every parked car. He felt exposed, like a target was pinned squarely between his shoulder blades.

A man in a hoodie paused to film them—Jude tensed, one hand going to Ella's back, gently urging her faster.

Behind them, the fire truck came roaring around the corner, lights flashing, tires screeching as it skidded to a stop. The chaos intensified. People were yelling, a woman crying, bystanders pointing toward the shop.

A second emergency vehicle pulled in behind the fire truck, its engine growling like a beast.

"Keep moving," Chen barked over the noise, staying tight to their side, one hand on the holster at her hip. "Get in your vehicle and go straight to the station. I'll be right behind you."

As they reached Jude's truck, Ella hesitated, glancing over her shoulder.

A low sound, almost a whimper, escaped her lips at the sight of her storefront—still standing, but wounded.

Jude opened the passenger door and gently guided her inside, shielding her with his body the entire time.

"Get in. Stay low," he said.

With a solemn look and a small nod, she slid inside and

shut the door. Her hands were shaking as she buckled her seat belt.

Jude rounded the truck, his jaw clenched, his blood humming with adrenaline. When he got behind the wheel, he locked the doors and looked at Ella—she was pale, drawn, but still upright. Still fighting.

The sight of her sitting there, hands trembling, breathing shallow, but refusing to fall apart—it hit him harder than the blast had. She hadn't run. She hadn't broken. The same stubborn spirit that once made him love her was still burning bright, no matter how much she'd forgotten.

He pulled away his gaze, tightening his grip on the wheel.

"Let's get out of here," he muttered.

And he drove, one eye on the road and the other on the rearview mirror, watching for a tail they couldn't afford to miss.

Ella sat stiffly in the passenger seat of Jude's truck, the seat belt tight across her chest like a vise as Jude pulled into the police-station parking lot. Her pulse thudded in her ears. Her hands trembled in her lap, but she pressed them together, willing herself to be steady. Her shop—her life—had been severely damaged by fire and smoke, and now she was about to face questions she had no answers to.

He waited for Detective Chen to park, then she met Ella at the passenger door. The two of them flanked her into the building, where they were met just inside the doors by the police chief, Gus Zimmerman.

The chief's posture was casual, almost too casual, as if he was simply waiting to chat with a friend rather than dealing with a crime scene involving a bombing. Ella noticed Jude clench his jaw, as if the sight of the duo annoyed him, but he said nothing.

Zimmerman broke into a wide, easy grin. "Well, if it isn't the hero of the day," he said jovially, striding toward them and clapping Jude hard on the shoulder. "Heard you saved the lady from becoming kindling. Good work, son."

Jude gave a stiff smile. "Just did what anyone would've done, sir."

Ella felt Jude tense, and not from modesty. There was something strained under the surface, something maybe only she would notice. She had to assume that Jude held a grudge toward Chief Zimmerman the same way he did toward Detective Chen.

Zimmerman's grin widened. "You always were a good kid, Jude. Just like your father. Man had a backbone and a heart. You take after him."

A shadow flickered across Jude's face, there and gone in an instant. Ella felt it like a shift in the air—grief, guilt, something raw and deep.

"He'd be proud of you, kid, following in his footsteps and becoming a game warden, too."

Jude's lips only offered up a pinched smile. Ella had to assume Jude didn't appreciate the so-called compliment. He was thirty, hardly a kid, and she was sure Jude considered Chief Zimmerman to be part of the botched murder investigation.

"Sounds like everything is under control?" Zimmerman said to Chen.

"Getting there," she said.

Chen stepped forward, her movements swift and smooth, her face politely blank. "Chief, I'll take it from here," she said coolly.

Zimmerman chuckled but didn't move. His gaze shifted to Ella, lingering a fraction too long. "You holding up okay, young lady?"

Ella summoned a polite smile. “I’m managing. Thank you.”

Chen subtly angled herself between Ella and the chief, her stance protective without being obvious. There was no mistaking it—beneath her professionalism, her entire body radiated tension.

Ella stiffened, feeling it but not understanding it.

“Jaclyn’s the best we’ve got,” Zimmerman said with a wink, addressing Jude as much as Ella. “She’ll get this sorted out.”

Jaclyn Chen’s expression didn’t change, but Ella caught it—a slight tightening around her eyes. A chill ran through her.

Zimmerman finally gave a lazy nod and strolled away, toward the front of the building.

The second he was out of earshot, Chen let out a slow breath. “Come on,” she said briskly, motioning them inside.

They entered through a side door into a small, plain conference room. The walls were beige and windowless. A scuffed table and ancient chairs filled the space.

Chen didn’t sit. She stayed standing, her posture sharp, as if still on the defensive.

“We’ll keep this short,” she said. “I got a call with an update. First off, the fire’s out since the department arrived almost immediately. Your shop sustained smoke and water damage, mostly contained to the back room. There’s significant damage to your office area. You’ll want to talk to your insurance adjuster to see what they recommend.”

Ella nodded numbly.

Chen continued, her voice clipped and efficient. “It appears the damage was from a homemade pipe bomb—unsophisticated but deadly. If you two hadn’t moved when you did…”

She didn’t finish the sentence. She didn’t need to.

"We'll be pulling security footage from businesses on the block," Chen said. "If you remember anything, and I mean anything, call me. Even a gut feeling. Even something that doesn't make sense."

Ella nodded, feeling as fragile as a blown-glass ornament about to shatter.

Chen's gaze softened briefly. "And just…be careful. Both of you. Not everyone who smiles at you is your friend."

The words hung there, heavy, and Ella felt they were full of meaning she wasn't quite grasping.

Ella didn't know how to respond. She glanced at Jude, who gave a small, sharp nod, understanding the warning without needing it spelled out.

"I'm sorry I asked you to meet me there," she said curtly. "I never imagined it would put you in danger. I had just hoped that walking through your shop would maybe strike up a memory."

Chen's expression was grim, and Ella knew the woman felt a needling of guilt.

"You couldn't have known," she said.

Jude's expression remained stoic and he said nothing.

"That's it for now. You're free to go."

Jude guided Ella out with a light hand on her back. The cool air hit her like a splash of water. She sucked in a shaky breath and tried to gather herself as they crossed the lot to his truck.

The entire interaction with Chief Zimmerman and Detective Chen buzzed in her mind like static on an old, outdated clock radio. Something about the way Chen had shifted between her and Zimmerman, something about the way Jude stiffened at the mention of his father—

It all felt…wrong.

But her memory remained stubbornly blank.

As Jude unlocked the truck and opened the door for her, she caught the way his jaw tightened, his gaze sweeping the shadows along the perimeter of the parking lot.

He hadn't missed the tension, either.

They climbed into the cab, locking the doors.

Jude gripped the steering wheel tighter than necessary, the leather creaking faintly beneath his fingers. For a long moment, he didn't start the engine. Ella felt she should say something, but she wasn't sure what. It was clear that the chief had stirred up old, awful feelings about Landon Sheridan's death. At one time, she would've known the right thing to say. Now, she felt as though she and Jude were on the verge of being strangers.

Still, she had to ask.

"Was Chief Zimmerman part of the investigation? Into your father's death, I mean?"

He gave her a quick look, then shook his head. "No. Not that I'm aware of. He wasn't chief at that time. He was on the force, an officer, I think, but I don't really remember him."

"Oh. Did you sense the tension between Zimmerman and Chen?"

"I sure did. It's hard to say what that was about. Probably interdepartmental politics of some sort."

"Right." Ella didn't know what to say, other than to simply agree. Jude was in law enforcement, so he'd have a better understanding than she did.

He finally turned the key, the truck rumbling to life. He slid a glance at Ella and she gave him a sympathetic smile that she hoped offered encouragement.

Whatever was coming, they weren't out of danger. Today had made that clear.

It was the third attempt. The third time someone had tried to kill her.

And she still didn't know who, or why.

Jude's voice broke through the silence. "We should just go to the clinic." Concern threaded every syllable. "It's almost time for your appointment."

Ella didn't argue. Nor did she argue when Jude insisted on accompanying her inside. Her regular doctor, Dr. Ingalls, looked her over, lightly chastising Ella for leaving the hospital, but didn't insist on sending her back. All in all, she concurred with what Dr. Andres had told Ella the night before. Post-traumatic retrograde amnesia, get rest, don't stress. Come back in a week since she insisted a hospital stay was out of the question.

Don't stress. Right, Ella thought as she climbed back into Jude's truck.

As he pulled away from the curb and headed to the ranch, she couldn't help but replay the explosion in her mind.

She'd felt his presence at her back, steady, unyielding. Protective. He had shielded her body with his.

"You didn't have to do that," she said quietly. "Protect me like that back at my shop."

"Yeah, I did," he answered, eyes still on the road. "I'm not letting anything happen to you. Not again."

The rest of the ride back to the ranch passed in tense silence. Ella watched the trees blur past, the familiar ache in her chest returning. It was part confusion, part guilt, all tangled with fear.

She also couldn't shake the image of the chief's lingering smile, the strange weight of Chen's warning.

Something about it tugged at the empty places in her mind.

Something important.

Something dangerous.

But the harder she chased it, the farther it slipped away.

Lexie's car was parked near the barn when they pulled in.

She hesitated for half a beat, bracing herself. Her legs were shaky, her head heavy, but she pushed forward. Jude brushed a hand lightly across her lower back as they walked up the steps of his wraparound porch.

A raspy meow was followed by a thump as Bandit jumped from his perch on the porch rafters. He landed on the log railing, then another hop landed him on the planks by her feet. She leaned down and scooped him up.

The cat immediately began to purr. She glanced at Jude, who tried to look annoyed but the slight smirk gave away his amusement as he opened the door.

The house smelled like baking bread and beef stew. Safe. Too safe, considering what had just happened.

"I need to make a call," Jude said after a beat. "Go ahead and get settled."

Ella nodded, her gaze following him as he disappeared down the hallway. She barely had time to exhale before Lexie stepped out of the kitchen, blocking the doorway, arms crossed.

They stared at each other in silence, the air thick with unspoken things.

Lexie was the first to speak. "I thought I knew you," she said. "But that was before you hurt Jude. That was before you cut both of us out of your life."

Ella drew in a breath, sending up a silent prayer for strength.

"I wish I had an explanation for that," she said, her voice softer than she intended. "But I don't. I'm as puzzled as you two are."

Lexie studied her with open suspicion. Then, slowly, her shoulders slumped, and her gaze dimmed with something closer to defeat than anger. Ella noticed then the deep weariness in Lexie's posture—like she'd been carrying too much hurt for too long.

"Do us all a favor, okay? Don't make Jude fall in love with you all over again. I can't fathom why you broke his heart the way you did, but what if you get your memory back, decide he's not right for you, and crush him all over again?"

"I wouldn't," Ella murmured, but her words held no weight. Not even to her own ears.

Lexie scowled. "Except we both know you already did."

Silence stretched, and Ella could offer nothing in return. She didn't have the answers. Just blank spaces in her mind and a growing fear that the past might hurt more than the present.

"Promise me something?" Lexie asked, her voice suddenly quieter but no less firm.

Ella hesitated. She already knew what was coming, but she asked, anyway. "What?"

"Keep some emotional distance between you and my brother. I get that you're here because he wants to keep you safe. That's who he is. It's what he does."

Ella bit her lip because she knew that Lexie was right. The pasture full of retired horses and this old, decrepit cat were a testament to that. As was his job. He was a game warden because someone had to keep watch. Over the land. Over the wildlife. Whether it was apprehending a poacher or coaxing a panicked deer out of a frozen creek, Jude had a way of stepping in and doing the hard things with steady hands and quiet resolve. He took care of things. Including her. It didn't mean anything. As Lexie had just pointed out, it was simply who he was. What he did.

"But let it go at that. Please," Lexie implored. "Let him take care of you if that's what he thinks he needs to do, but don't make him fall in love with you again. I was here when he picked up the pieces. He didn't deserve that. And he definitely doesn't deserve to go through it again."

"If I ended our engagement, I must've had a good reason," Ella said, the words tasting hollow even as they left her lips.

"And what happens when you remember that oh-so-important reason?" Lexie asked, a note of frustration creeping in.

Ella met her gaze evenly, though a lump had formed in her throat. "Nothing will happen. It's already over between us."

But why did that feel like a lie?

And if it had been her choice, why did it hurt so much?

Lexie seemed satisfied with that. "Good. Make sure you keep it that way." She turned on her heel, headed toward the fridge and pulled it open without another word.

Ella stood frozen, the weight of the conversation pressing on her chest. Her heart thudded painfully as Jude's footsteps echoed from the hallway. He stepped into the kitchen, his gaze flicking between them.

"What's that about?" he asked, looking directly at her.

Ella's lips parted, then closed. She shook her head lightly. "Nothing," she said.

Jude's eyebrows pinched slightly, a flicker of doubt crossing his face, but he let it go.

But she knew the truth.

It was everything.

And nothing she said could make any of it okay.

The fact that Jude was letting her stay here, despite the way she'd hurt him, only drove home how much danger she was really in.

FIVE

The next morning, Ella awoke relieved to find that the throbbing in her head had subsided. Mostly. There was still an echo of a dull ache. But it was much more tolerable than it had been. The nausea had finally diminished as well, and she realized she was ravenous.

The scent of something sweet, waffles or pancakes, crept into her room. She was almost fooled into thinking it was a normal morning. Almost.

But normal didn't exist anymore. Not when someone had tried to kill her. Twice. No, three times now. Not when shadows clung to every missing piece of her memory like secrets she wasn't ready to uncover.

The thought of staying in bed for a while longer, nestled cozily under the covers, was tempting. Knowing that Lexie or Jude, or probably both, were already awake got her moving. Lexie had stayed the night again, claiming that the part to fix her furnace was on back order.

It didn't feel safe to stay in bed, ignoring reality, when there were potential murderers on the loose.

She tossed the covers off and quickly slid into a pair of jeans and a plain white long-sleeved T-shirt. Before leaving her house yesterday, she'd packed a small suitcase. It felt good to be in her own clothes again. She wrangled her hair into a ponytail as she walked down the steps. The clanging of pots and running of water from the kitchen apparently drowned out her approach, but not the sound of the siblings' voices.

She didn't mean to eavesdrop as she made her descent, but it couldn't be helped. They weren't exactly whispering.

"She's not your responsibility, Jude," Lexie said.

"I know that," Jude replied. "But what was I supposed to do? She has nowhere to go. I can't just dump her off on her parents. What if they tracked her there? You know her dad's health is declining. Her mom has her hands full taking care of him. Ella doesn't want to put her friends at risk." He paused, then repeated, "What was I supposed to do?"

"Let her figure it out!" Lexie said. "Her life is not your concern."

"Lexie," Jude growled, "enough. You need to remember that whoever is after her, they mean business. They want her dead. I might not be real excited to have her in my house, but I'm not going to let that get in the way of trying to keep her alive."

"You're right," Lexie muttered, sounding chagrined. "I need to remember to look at the big picture here. She's only here because you've taken pity on her."

Ella instinctively flinched at the truth of Lexie's words.

She paused at the bottom of the stairs, heart hammering, the ugly reality slamming into her chest. She wasn't family. She wasn't even a friend anymore. She was a liability they were trying to protect and barely tolerating.

She reached the kitchen and hurried inside, not wanting to hear Jude's response because she knew Lexie was right in her assertion.

She was only there because Jude, with his kind heart, had taken pity on her.

It was a humbling, and melancholy, thought.

"Good morning," she said, forcing some cheer into her tone. Her voice came out too brightly, almost brittle.

The last thing she wanted was for them to realize that she'd overheard. None of them needed that awkwardness first thing in the morning. Or ever.

"The pancakes smell wonderful. Can I do anything to help?"

Jude gave her a quizzical, assessing look, and despite the smile she wore, Ella knew that he knew she'd heard. He ducked his head and clenched his jaw as he sliced the rest of the strawberries that were in the strainer.

"We just finished eating," Lexie said. "But you go ahead and help yourself. I need to hustle or I'm going to be late for work. We're getting a big group for a wedding this weekend." She turned to Jude. "I'll be back around dinnertime. Do you want me to bring pizza?"

"Sure," he agreed.

Lexie flounced out of the kitchen, ignoring Ella as she went.

The front door slammed shut and Ella sighed. "I feel like she hates me."

Jude's lips twitched in the hint of a smile. "Nah. She's just young and doesn't really seem to grasp the seriousness of the situation."

She was twenty-six. Not that young, but Ella was in no position to argue.

"She's also pretty protective of her big brother," Ella said.

"That, too." He motioned for her to sit, so she complied. "I'm sorry. I assume you heard us talking."

Ella waved a dismissive hand. She did not want to dwell on it. "It's fine. She's right. You've taken me in because you've taken pity on me. Just like Clementine and Ramona."

He snorted a half laugh. "Ella. I adore those two horses, but despite what's happened between us, you'll always mean more to me than any equine."

"Right. Okay. Can we just pretend I didn't hear what Lexie said?"

"Sure. Did you sleep okay?" He moved about the kitchen, dishing up some pancakes for her as they talked.

"I did, thank you."

Jude set the plate in front of her, along with a bottle of pure maple syrup and strawberries. Next, he poured her a cup of juice.

Ella could feel the tension building in the air, coiling tighter, heavier, like the room itself was bracing for something.

Jude sat across from her, fidgeting, occasionally sipping his coffee, spinning the cup around and around on the table.

"Okay," Ella said as she pushed away her half-eaten plate. "What is it?"

"What?" Jude's hands stilled, freezing his tottering coffee cup in place.

"You're antsy. You seem like you want to say something."

He emitted a frustrated, deep sigh. "I keep wondering if you were in trouble all those months ago. I wonder if there was something I could've done to help but maybe I misread the signs."

Her brow furrowed. "I don't understand."

He winced. "One day, out of the blue, it seemed like you didn't want to spend time with me anymore. When we were together, you were tense and just seemed really unhappy. I tried to talk to you about it, but you just became more withdrawn." He shrugged and winced. "Honestly, I thought maybe you were cheating on me."

She gasped, truly startled by his claim. "Jude! That's a horrible thing to say!"

He shrugged but had the good sense to look chagrined. "What was I supposed to think?"

"That I would never," she said.

He arched an eyebrow. "You don't know that. You don't know anything about those missing months."

"That's true. But I do know myself. I know my standards, my morals."

"Okay, so maybe you met someone else," he persisted. "And broke it off with me before starting a new relationship."

"I don't think so." Her chest tightened at the thought. It didn't fit—none of it fit.

She didn't think so, but she couldn't guarantee it. There was no denying that her feelings toward Jude had shifted, but in an undefinable way.

"But wait… You said you might have misread the signs. What do you mean?"

"Now, I'm wondering if you were in trouble even back then." He paused, then said, "And maybe you didn't feel comfortable asking me for help." He raked a hand through his hair. "If that's the case, you should've been able to come to me."

Ella resisted the urge to clasp Jude's hand in hers. "We don't know that's what happened."

"Right," he agreed. "Because we don't know anything."

For a heartbeat, the weight of everything unspoken hung between them. The missing months. The danger she didn't remember inviting. The cold certainty that whoever wanted her dead wasn't finished yet.

Ella pushed away from the table, grabbed her dirty dishes and rinsed them in the sink. She spoke as she worked. "I'm going to make a few phone calls."

"To who? Your parents?"

"I checked in with them already. I told them about the accident, but not about the amnesia or my shop. I'm grateful they don't have any connections to Haven Creek, because I'd like to shield them from this as much as possible until we have some answers."

She didn't want their worry, their panic, to echo her own. "But I need to call Julie and Stacey. I missed calls from both of them yesterday. I'm sure they heard about the accident and that they were checking in. I should've called them back then, but I wasn't feeling up to it so I put it off. They're my best friends so if I would've confided in anyone, it would likely be them."

He nodded. "You go do that. I'll clean the kitchen. Then we'll make a game plan for today."

She cocked her head to the side. "Game plan?"

He nodded. "I think I should do some digging around on my own."

"Um? Just you? No, I don't think so. What about me? This is my mess."

"And you are under doctor's orders to relax."

True.

But if she couldn't dig around, then neither should he.

"Detective Chen is on the case. You don't think we should just let her do her job?"

His jaw hardened. Ella noticed how his knuckles whitened around his coffee cup, another flash of the depth of his old pain. "You know how well that worked out for my family." His voice was low. Tight. Pain flashed across his face. Clearly, meeting with the detective yesterday scraped open some old emotional wounds.

"Oh, Jude. I'm sorry."

He waved her away. "It's not your fault. Go make your phone calls."

"Do you want to talk about it? Your dad, I mean?"

"No. I really don't." Jude took his cup and brought it to the sink.

Fifteen minutes later, Ella rejoined Jude in the kitchen.

One glance at her face and he asked, "Any leads?"

"None," Ella agreed. She had called her two closest friends, aside from Lexie, to ask if they had any insight into what she'd been up to the past few months. They were both shocked by the amnesia, but also readily acknowledged that she'd been distant for quite some time. Both had attributed her dour mood to her breakup with Jude. Her two closest friends had sounded surprised to hear from her and both admitted that she had almost completely frozen them out.

She clenched the phone in her hand, a quiet dread settling in her chest. She had broken up with Jude, and Lexie had shut her out because of it. But why would she have distanced herself from Stacey and Julie? They had been her friends for years.

Unless it hadn't just been about Jude. Unless something bigger had been driving her away from everyone she loved.

Apprehension zipped down her spine, sharp and cold.

What, oh, what, did those missing months hold?

Ella sighed as Jude pulled up to her house.

"Are you sure you want to do this?" he asked.

"Want to?" She scoffed. "No. But I need to. My house isn't going to clean itself. I'm not supposed to stress, but the thought of this mess is giving me heart palpitations." She turned to face him. "I appreciate the ride, but you don't need to stay with me."

He shrugged. "I don't have to go into work. What else am I going to do?"

The truth was, whether he had something else to do or not, he wasn't about to leave Ella's side. He didn't want to tell her that. Didn't want her reading too much into it. Helping out, having someone's back—it was something he'd do for any one of his friends.

Especially someone still recovering from a concussion and amnesia.

She insisted she had to do something, not just sit around and wait. She couldn't exactly catch a criminal, but she could get her house back in order. And he would be there—to do the bulk of the work while making sure she took it easy. In fact, once they were inside, he was going to insist she kick her feet up and relax. Maybe read a book or watch a movie while he dealt with the destruction from the intruder.

Then, when the attackers were caught, she could return to a clean house—and they could go their separate ways once again.

If only it was that simple.

Nothing about this situation—her memory loss, the attacks, their shared past—was simple anymore.

"It's nothing," he said when she thanked him. "Don't worry about it."

He didn't want to admit that spending time with her was twisting his heart into a knot all over again.

"Let's get in there and get this done," he said.

They slid from the truck and made their way up the sidewalk. Ella was a few steps ahead, climbing the porch stairs, when she suddenly whirled around, her eyes wide, her hand clamping hard on his arm.

"What?" he demanded, his pulse spiking.

"The door," she whispered. "It's open. We didn't leave it open."

His gaze swung to the house. The screen door was shut, but the blue entry door behind it was wide open.

She was right. They hadn't left it that way.

Every instinct in him screamed that it was a trap.

For a breathless moment, the world seemed to freeze. The late-morning sun beat down on the cracked sidewalk, a light breeze stirred the bushes along the porch—all seemed normal and well. But was it?

"Get in the truck," he said quietly, pressing the keys into her hand. "Lock the doors. Take off if you have to."

Ella hesitated, her gaze swinging between the door and Jude.

"Let's both go," she whispered.

"Not yet." What if this was their best chance, maybe their only chance, to catch whoever was behind this?

"I'm going in. You need to get back in the truck, where it's safer."

"You're not going in there alone," she argued.

"I have a weapon. You have a concussion. Please, Ella. Call the police. I might need backup. Now, go."

For a heartbeat, he thought she would argue again.

Then she turned and darted down the steps, sprinting for the truck.

Only when he saw her get inside and lock the doors did he move.

He drew his weapon, keeping low.

They hadn't exactly been subtle driving up with doors slamming and engine rumbling. No stealth.

He hated the idea of waiting for backup and giving whoever was inside time to escape. Not this time.

The screen door creaked open under his hand. Jude stepped inside, gun raised, all his senses on high alert.

The air inside smelled wrong. A faint whiff of something flowery, perhaps perfume, with the lingering stench of spoiled milk from the wrecked kitchen. Jude's boots crunched lightly on broken glass scattered across the entryway. He winced, but there was no helping it now.

A thud from the back of the house snapped his attention forward. The intruder hadn't even bothered to be quiet.

Footsteps. A drawer slamming. Closet doors sliding open and shut.

He moved soundlessly across the living room, sticking to the wall, scanning every shadow, checking behind him in case it was a setup.

God, please guide me. Keep Ella safe. Keep me sharp.

As he approached the hallway, he saw it, a shadow moving across the bedroom wall.

There was no doubt now—someone was still inside.

He crept to the doorway, swung in, gun trained—

"Hands up!" he barked.

The figure turned.

His heart slammed against his ribs.

Stacey.

She shrieked, earbuds tumbling from her ears as she slapped a hand over her chest. "Jude! You nearly scared me to death!"

That made two of them.

He holstered his weapon and exhaled sharply. "Yeah. Same. I better call off the cavalry because I'm sure Ella just called them in from my truck."

He pulled out his phone while Stacey apologized and offered to explain everything to the 911 dispatcher.

When Jude returned to the front of the house, Ella came barging through the front door, where Stacey was waving to her.

"Stacey!" she cried, rushing forward. "What are you doing here?"

Her friend gave a sheepish shrug. "Julie and I felt terrible after hearing what happened. We wanted to help."

She motioned toward the living room.

It was cleaner. Straighter. The chaos from before had lessened noticeably.

"I remembered I still had a key from when I watered your plants last summer, when you went to visit your parents for a week. We figured we'd clean things up for you."

Ella frowned. "I didn't see your car."

"Julie's at the store grabbing groceries to replace the ones that were destroyed. I stayed to work on your house." Stacey smiled warmly. "I didn't mean to scare you."

Ella's gaze swept the room, her face softening. "Thank you. I can't believe you guys went to all this trouble."

"That's what friends are for." Stacey squeezed her hands gently. "How are you doing, for real?"

Ella flicked a glance at Jude, then back to Stacey. "I'm okay."

Jude stepped closer, seizing the moment. "Actually, mind if we ask you something?"

"Of course." Stacey nodded.

"I know you said I shut you out, but is there anything you remember?" Ella asked.

"I might know something," she said. "I've been thinking about our conversation, ever since we got off the phone this morning. A few months ago, I came to your shop. Marjorie was working up front and said you were in your office, but when I peeked in, it was empty. Then I heard you—outside. Through the open window. You were arguing with someone in the alley."

"Who?" Jude asked.

Stacey hesitated. "I don't know. Just that I heard a woman's voice."

Jude's gut twisted. The attacker in the hospital had been a male...hadn't he? And the driver of the truck? But everything had happened so fast. Had Jude just assumed? No. He wasn't trying to be sexist, but that punch he'd taken to the jaw? Well, he was pretty sure there was a whole lot of manpower behind it.

"She had her back to me," Stacey said. "Average build. Athletic. Black hair. I didn't recognize her."

Ella shook her head slowly. "I can't think of who that could be."

"You said something about being tired of deception," Stacey added. "And she said lives are on the line—and that you needed to step up your game."

Jude stiffened.

Lives are on the line.

That wasn't just an argument.

It was a warning.

"You're sure you don't know who it was?" Jude asked again.

"I'm sure." Stacey glanced at Ella with real regret. "Afterward, you begged me not to tell anyone. You said if I cared about our friendship, I'd forget it."

Ella visibly paled.

Jude felt it, too—that dark puzzle piece sliding into place.

Ella hadn't just distanced herself.

She'd been hiding something.

Stacey apologized again, but Jude barely heard. His mind was racing ahead.

"We need to find out who that woman was," he said grimly.

Ella's face was pale but determined. "Marjorie. She might know."

Marjorie was her part-time worker who helped around the shop so Ella was able to get away occasionally.

"You go talk to her," Stacey encouraged. "Julie should be back any minute. We'll finish up here."

"Thank you," Ella said, her words heartfelt.

They moved toward the door—and Jude's instincts flared again.

His hand brushed Ella's back lightly, guiding her. They were halfway out the door when he spotted it—

A flash of metal.

Between two houses across the street.

A man. Crouched low. Rifle raised.

"Ella," he said, voice low and sharp, "get down."

She dropped to her knees.

Crack!

The shot rang out, loud and violent.

Jude grabbed her and yanked her backward, both of them crashing to the floor inside the doorway.

Another bullet ripped through the doorframe, sending splinters flying.

"Stay down!" Jude barked, already rolling to the side, drawing his weapon.

Through the cracked door he saw the gunman sprinting and then he vanished between houses.

Too late.

He slammed the door shut and threw the dead bolt.

When he turned, Ella was sitting against the wall, her breathing shallow, her hands trembling.

"You okay?" he asked, crouching beside her.

She nodded numbly.

Her voice came out a ragged whisper. "That shot…it was for me."

Jude's jaw tightened.

He put a steadying hand on her shoulder.

"Yeah. It was."

Stacey peeked around the corner, her eyes wide and terrified. "Did someone just shoot at you?"

"They did," Jude affirmed.

And whoever was behind it wasn't finished.

SIX

Ella gripped her hands tightly in her lap, her heart still hammering from their near miss earlier. They had been shot at. Someone had fired real bullets at them. The reality of it weighed heavily on her chest, the pain sharp and suffocating. She couldn't shake the guilt gnawing at her insides. Jude and Stacey could have been hurt, killed, all because of her. If anything happened to either of them, she would never forgive herself.

Detective Chen had been notified, and there were officers scouring the area after the trio had given their statements, but it seemed at this point, the shooter was going to get away once again.

She dragged in a slow, calming breath and tried to focus. They were on their way to do some investigating, chase the few leads they had. She had to keep her mind clear. Jude was risking his life to help her, and she needed to be strong.

Ella had nearly wept with gratitude when she realized the amount of effort her friends had put into cleaning her house. She felt blessed to have the two of them in her life. Despite all that had gone wrong the last few days, she knew she needed to focus on all that was right. She had wonderful friends. She was safe, for the moment. And she had Jude by her side, trying to solve this mystery with her. She didn't want to think of what would happen when this was over, but the thought was never far from her mind.

Would he walk away, without looking back?

If he did, could she blame him?

Or after all of this, would they find their way back to each other?

Is that what she wanted? She didn't know. She still had no recollection of why she'd returned her ring. And what if Lexie was right and her memory came back? What if she realized it hadn't been a mistake to leave Jude?

That reminded her of the promise she had made to Jude's sister. She needed to banish any thought other than friendship from her mind.

She fought down a growl of frustration. Not knowing why she broke off their engagement was almost as maddening as not knowing who wanted to kill her.

As Jude drove toward Marjorie's home, she forced her mind back to what they had learned from Stacey.

"I hope Marjorie can shed some light on this situation," Ella said. "When I spoke with her yesterday to let her know about my accident and the fire, I didn't think to ask if she knew anything that might help me. At the time, I really didn't know what kind of information I was looking for."

Marjorie Fossen had owned a consignment store in town for nearly three decades. Two years ago, she sold it so she could retire. It hadn't taken her long to realize retirement didn't really suit her. While chatting with Ella at church one day, Marjorie had shared her tales of boredom. Ella, needing some part-time help at her store, had made an offer Marjorie had been delighted over. She began helping Ella, filling in so Ella could attend estate sales, work in the office, or just run a few errands.

"Since she covers for you at work, and sees you several

times a week, she'd be able to tell us better than anyone if she thought you'd been up to something. Or if someone had been visiting since she works the floor while you do book-work," Jude said. As he made the final turn leading to Marjorie's house, he asked, "You don't have any idea who this woman may be that you were arguing with?"

"Not really." She heaved a weary sigh. "I mean, I can't think of that many women with that hair color. And the ones that do come to mind don't fit the description. One has a pixie cut, the other is tall and willowy, not really athletically built. I guess it could be a customer."

"A customer angry enough to be speaking of life-and-death matters?" Jude asked.

"Your guess is as good as mine."

As they turned down Marjorie's quiet street, a prickle crawled up Ella's spine. A dark sedan sat idling at the far end of the block. Jude noticed it, too. She could tell by the way his jaw tightened. He slowed, watching the car in his rearview mirror even after they passed it. The engine revved once—a low, guttural sound—and then fell silent again. Whoever was inside wasn't moving. But were they watching? Or did they belong there?

She'd never been a paranoid person. Now, she felt suspicious of nearly everything. She supposed murder attempts were bound to do that to someone.

They parked in front of the small, neatly kept gray home. The house was lined with flowerbeds, the flowers now waning this time of year, but Ella knew they were beautiful when in full bloom. Which they had been during the summer.

The last of the days she could remember.

Frustration surged again and she tried to tamp it down.

Marjorie's eyes lit up when she opened the door and found Ella on her porch. She pulled Ella into a grandmotherly hug.

"I'm so happy to see you. I've been so worried. I can't stop thinking about your lovely shop. Destroyed! It's awful. Just awful." She released Ella, searching her eyes for answers. "Who would do such a thing?"

Jude cleared his throat, and Marjorie seemed to notice him for the first time. "Well, ma'am, we're hoping you might be able to help us with that."

She refused to answer a single question until she had seated them at the table, with glasses of lemonade, and a full update on what had happened to Ella over the past few days. When Ella finished the condensed version of her ordeal, she said, "I'm hoping you can help me piece the last few months together."

"I'll do what I can," Marjorie assured her. "What would you like to know?"

Ella glanced at Jude. He gave her an encouraging nod. On the ride over they'd discussed the questions Ella should ask.

"Can you tell me about my routine the past few months?"

"For the most part, it was the same as it's always been." She hesitated, thinking something over. "You left every Tuesday morning for your ten o'clock Bible study, just like always. I'm not sure what you did after, but Bible study only lasts an hour and you were always gone for two or three. That was new."

Ella mulled that over. Could Bible study be a clue? How could Bible study and her attackers possibly be related?

"Maybe you never went to Bible study," Jude offered.

He was met with disgruntled looks from both Ella and Marjorie.

"I wouldn't lie about going to Bible study," Ella huffed.

Jude shrugged. "It was just a thought. Since no one seems to know what you were up to lately."

She ignored the comment and returned her attention to Marjorie. "Have I been acting strange lately?"

Marjorie frowned, cutting her gaze to Jude and then back to Ella. "I won't lie. You've been a little off. Withdrawn. Agitated. Quieter than usual. To be honest," she continued, "I thought it had to do with your broken engagement. You told everyone that it was mutual. But I started to wonder if maybe he called it off, broke your heart, but thought he was doing you a favor by allowing you to say it was mutual." Her brow furrowed in consternation. "I had a hard time believing the mutual part. The way you walked around, all on edge and brokenhearted." She gave Jude a hard look, as if silently accusing him.

"Mutual?" Jude grumbled. "She ended things with me."

Marjorie frowned.

Ella did not like the turn this conversation had taken. The only reason she could think of saying the breakup was mutual was to spare Jude's dignity, because it was clear he hadn't wanted any part of the breakup.

At least not then. He seemed to be over her now, and was offering his protection, but maintaining the emotional distance his sister requested.

"Is there anything else you can think of?" she asked. "Did I have any visitors?"

"Just the usual ones, as far as I can recall," Marjorie said. "The regulars who stop by, hoping you'll sell some of their items on commission. Your usual group of friends who drop in to chat. You know—" her brow furrowed "—come to think of it, there is something. I don't know if it's important or not."

Ella leaned forward in expectation.

"You started taking a phone call every Wednesday promptly at noon. Could that be important?" Marjorie asked.

"Possibly," Ella said. "Any idea who I was speaking with?"

"No, dear. I'm sorry. I can tell you it was a bit unusual, though. You always seemed a bit high-strung over the calls. You would go in your office and lock the door."

Ella's brow furrowed. "I never lock my door."

"That's why I found it unusual. I only noticed because a few times I was standing near enough that I heard the lock click into place."

Ella shivered, unease creeping along her skin. She imagined herself locking the door, holding whispered conversations with a stranger. She didn't recognize the version of herself Marjorie described. That terrified her more than anything else.

Ella and Jude exchanged curious glances. Could this be important? If so, how? Ella needed to check her phone for past incoming calls.

"I'm sorry I couldn't be of more help," Marjorie said. "I really can't think of anything else."

"I do have one more question," Ella said. She reiterated the description Stacey had given her. "Do you have any idea who that might be? Do you recall her coming in?"

Marjorie shook her head. "I don't. But we have a lot of customers, as you know." She pursed her lips, pausing while lost in thought. "I don't suppose you remember Annette Ballenger? The name stuck in my head because my grandson had a teacher, Allen Ballenger, and I wondered if it was his wife. It's not a very common name," she said as an aside. "And she was middle-aged, just like Allen."

Ella slowly shook her head, hoping the name would spark in her memory if she gave it some time. "No. I don't. Who is she?"

"She was an angry customer. She could fit the description," Marjorie said.

"What was she angry about?" Ella couldn't fathom someone being upset enough about a transaction to turn it into a life-and-death matter, but there were people in the world who definitely had their own way of thinking.

"She brought in a gold-coin set. You offered to take them on consignment, but she wanted you to buy them outright." Marjorie frowned. "I got the very distinct impression that she really needed the cash. However, the price she wanted was outrageous. Of course, you told her so. Not in so many words, you were very polite. But she became extremely hostile toward you. She finally left but she did say that you would regret not taking her up on her offer. I thought she meant that you'd change your mind. But—"

"But maybe she meant she'd make Ella regret it," Jude interrupted.

"She did seem desperate for cash," Marjorie added. "I know people can do some terrible things when they feel desperate."

"Is she from town?" Ella asked.

"I do believe so," Marjorie said.

They were silent a few moments, mulling that over. Ella was mentally trying to poke a hole in the dam that held back her memory. Marjorie looked as if she was lost in contemplation as well, likely trying to recall anything else of import.

"Well," Jude said as he got up, "thank you for your time. Please let us know if you think of anything else."

"Yes, thank you," Ella said. "This information might be useful. I'm just not sure yet."

As they left, Ella couldn't shake the feeling they were being watched. She turned once to glance behind them but there was no one there.

Jude couldn't help but listen to Ella's phone call as he drove, his hand tightening on the steering wheel, every instinct on alert. He didn't know what to think when Marjorie had nearly accused him of breaking Ella's heart. Yeah. Right. If only she knew the truth, but no sense going there.

He'd certainly hoped for something more useful, but it sounded as if Ella had been reclusive the last few months, so it only made sense that Marjorie didn't have much more to offer than Ella's friends had.

He caught the tail end of her conversation.

"Okay, thanks, Joanne. I appreciate the prayers. We'll talk soon." Ella disconnected the call and dropped her phone back into her purse. "Apparently I've really hit it off with Madison Zimmerman."

"The police chief's daughter?" Jude asked, his voice low, sharp with disbelief.

"Stepdaughter," she absently corrected, "but yes."

Okay. Stepdaughter. That didn't jibe with the scenarios that had been running through his mind. He'd half convinced himself that Ella had gotten herself tangled in something illegal. Gunfire didn't just happen without a reason. Being shot at didn't seem like it could have anything at all to do with her new best friend. Madison, from what he could recall of her, was quiet. Shy. And quite a bit younger than Ella. If he had to guess, he'd say she was still in college.

Closer to Lexie's age.

"She said we went out for lunch at Rocky's Café, every Tuesday without fail. That would explain the delay in returning to my shop after Bible study."

Jude glanced in his rearview mirror, determined the lane was clear, flipped on his blinker and cut over more aggressively than usual, making Ella tense.

"What are you doing?" Ella asked, her voice edged with wariness.

"We're going to get some lunch. At Rocky's. Your doctor

said it was impossible to tell what might trigger your memory. Maybe the coffee shop will. Why don't you try giving Madison a call?"

"I have her number in my phone," Ella admitted. "I noticed it yesterday, but I didn't think anything of it. We exchanged numbers early last spring. She had asked if I would be interested in some of her mother's antiques. I had told her that, of course, I would. She never did call." Her brow creased. "Not that I remember, anyway. I knew she was struggling with her mother's dementia, so I didn't want to push. Oh!" she exclaimed, a flicker of realization crossing her face. "That has to be it."

"What?" Jude asked, suspicion curling low in his gut. "What's *it*?"

"The reason we've been hanging out. Maybe our parents' illness is the common thread. It would make sense. Her mom's been sick for a while but has begun to decline rapidly. And my dad, well, he's doing okay but it's still stressful. Between our parents and going to Bible study together, it makes sense we made a connection and started spending some time together."

Jude's stomach sank. "So it's another dead end." He shook his head. Whatever was going on, he didn't think Madison Zimmerman could be any part of it. She was the police chief's daughter. Her connection to Ella was through Bible study. On paper, it all sounded safe. Too safe.

He glanced over at Ella. She appeared lost in her thoughts.

"What's going through that mind of yours?" Jude asked, his voice quiet, wary.

She pinched the bridge of her nose and closed her eyes. "I wish I knew. I feel like everything I need to know is swimming around in my brain. Just out of reach. I keep mentally reaching for thoughts and it's like they just dart away."

"Don't press it," Jude warned, his tone firm, protective. "Remember what Dr. Ingalls said."

She let out a little growl of frustration as she let her head rest against the seat. "I know. But it's so hard! There's so much at stake. If I could just remember!"

"There's always a chance that even if you remembered, it wouldn't help."

"Maybe," she said, her voice low.

"You don't think so?" He tapped his hand against the steering wheel. "Why? What's making you think otherwise? What's your gut telling you?"

She pulled in a deep breath. Released it slowly.

In his field, he'd had to trust his gut instinct, intuition, a whisper from God, whatever you wanted to call it, more times than he could count. "If you can't trust your memories, maybe we need to listen to your instincts."

"I have this nagging feeling that my relationship with Madison..." She frowned, her voice dropping, the air thickening between them. "I feel like there's something not right with it. I'm not sure why. Or what. I can't really explain it. It feels off. But everything about the past few months seems off. So maybe I'm just transferring those feelings to Madison."

"Or maybe you're not," Jude said, his mind already racing through darker possibilities. "Always trust your instincts. Call her. See if you can get a feel for the situation."

The closer they got to Rocky's, the tighter the tension wound inside him. He caught himself scanning every car they passed, searching for windows that were darkly tinted, for a flash of metal, for anything that didn't sit right.

"It feels strange. Calling her, I mean. I've been friends with Julie and Stacey for a really long time. I have a history with them. Calling Madison, it feels so out of the blue. I feel like I barely know her. It's not like I'll be calling to just say hello. But 'hello, do you have any idea who might be trying to kill me?'" She threw her hands up, her frustration slicing the air like a blade.

Jude released a dry chuckle. "I get your point. However, we have limited options here."

"True," Ella muttered and made the call.

He could hear the phone ring. And ring. After several rings, voice mail kicked on.

"Hi, Madison. This is Ella Clarke. You may have heard that I was in an accident. My memory is a bit foggy right now. I, um, I'm wondering if you could give me a call? Maybe help me fill in a few blanks? Thanks so much," she said with forced cheer. "I look forward to hearing from you."

"I guess now we just wait," Jude said, every sense still humming with unease.

He cruised down the block, hoping that taking Ella out for lunch wasn't a huge mistake. But if this place could trigger a memory, it would be worth the risk. He maneuvered his truck into a parking spot in front of Rocky's, surprised when Ella's phone alerted them to a text. She glanced at the screen, and he peered at it, too.

Hi, Ella! I'm so sorry about your accident. I'm out of town camping for the week with some friends. I told you about it, but under the circumstances it sounds like you forgot. Reception is terrible here. I'll call you when I get back.

"If reception is so terrible," Jude said with a frown, his own instincts flaring in warning, "how was she able to hear your message?"

Ella shrugged. "Maybe she had to listen to it a few times.

Or maybe she's enjoying her time away with her friends and doesn't want to be disturbed."

Jude wasn't buying it. The knot in his stomach twisted tighter. Something about the timing didn't sit right. It felt too convenient. Too rehearsed. Like Madison had expected that call and already had her excuse ready.

Maybe, Jude thought, his jaw clenching. Or maybe she's hiding.

Either way, it didn't sound like they'd be hearing from Madison anytime soon.

SEVEN

The bell over the door jingled as Jude opened the door to Rocky's. Ella studied the place as she entered. She'd been there before, sure, but her last recollection of the café was of last winter, when she'd stopped for hot chocolate. In her memories, it wasn't a place she'd frequented.

Please, God, let this place jiggle some memories loose.

The young lady behind the counter grinned when she saw Ella. "Hello, would you like your usual?"

She had a usual? She supposed that made sense if she was here so often. She pasted on a smile, trying not to let on that she had no idea who this girl was, even though she apparently recognized Ella and her preferences.

"Yes, please," she said lightly. "That would be wonderful."

The cashier punched in her order before turning her attention to Jude. "And for you?"

He pulled his gaze from the short menu of soups, salads and sandwiches. "I'll just have whatever she's having."

"Sure thing."

They were given their total and Ella quickly paid for both meals. It was the very least she could do, considering all Jude had done for her the last few days.

"Your usual table is open. If you want to take a seat, we'll bring out your order when it's ready."

"And which table is that?" Jude asked, leaning forward and giving the young woman a charming smile.

She glanced at Ella. Ella could feel her questioning gaze but pretended to busy herself with putting her change away. She couldn't answer that question so she hoped her silence would encourage the cashier to answer Jude.

"The back-corner booth."

"Awesome," Jude said. "That's where we'll be."

His hand came to rest lightly against the small of Ella's back, but there was a new tension there, a subtle urgency as if he, too, felt the undercurrent of unease that had settled over them. She didn't want to think of how comforting his touch was. A wave of nostalgia washed over her.

She settled into the booth and looked around.

"Anything clicking into place?" Jude asked as he dropped into the seat across from her.

She shrugged. "I've been here before, so the place is familiar. But nothing jogs my memory."

Still, she couldn't shake the feeling that something was hovering just beyond reach. Like a faint memory, heavy and unsettling. If she had a usual order, she clearly came here often, likely with Madison, as she had been told. But why? And why did it feel as if the young woman was avoiding her? Especially when her message had sounded cheery, as if they were really friends.

As they waited, the door jangled again. Ella looked up to see Chief Zimmerman walk in, flanked by two uniformed officers. They were laughing about something, the chief's voice carrying easily over the low hum of conversation. When he caught sight of Jude, he strode over.

"Well, look what the cat dragged in," Zimmerman said with a caustic grin, clapping Jude on the shoulder a little too firmly. "Heard you got yourselves into a bit of trouble again.

You're really keeping Chen on her toes. She's got good instincts, but instincts can't replace real experience and we both know her track record isn't the best."

Ella blinked, startled by the casually disparaging remark. Jude's polite smile tightened, and Ella felt her own wariness spike.

For a moment, she considered mentioning her new friendship with Madison, his stepdaughter, but something about Zimmerman's easygoing manner made her throat tighten. A small, sharp warning bell rang in the back of her mind. She stayed silent.

"You two take care now," Zimmerman added, then headed to the counter.

Ella watched him go, unease coiling tighter in her gut.

There was something too casual in the chief's smile. Too dismissive when he spoke of Detective Chen.

She wasn't sure who unsettled her more now. Chen, with her clipped words and intense gaze that made Ella feel as if she'd done something wrong, or Zimmerman, with his easy grins that somehow felt like a mask?

All she knew for certain was that danger was getting harder to recognize.

She pulled out her phone. "While we're waiting for our meals, I'm going to check my call log."

There were several calls to the usual people in her life. Her parents, her friends, pizza delivery from her favorite pizzeria owned by an elderly couple who refused to go online. It came as no surprise that there were no recent calls to Jude, or Lexie. Still, the confirmation of the distance between them hurt.

"Anything?"

She shook her head. A few more swipes across her phone

brought her to what she was looking for. She sucked in a surprised breath and turned her phone for Jude to see.

"A call from a blocked number last Wednesday, just like Marjorie said."

She nodded and scrolled backward. "Another one, the Wednesday prior. And another." She continued to scroll, counting fourteen calls in all.

Jude rubbed his chin. His expression darkened.

"The calls precede our breakup then, by a few weeks."

"When we're done here, I'll call Detective Chen," Ella said. "Maybe she'll be able to have someone trace the calls."

Jude made a noncommittal sound, letting Ella know what he thought of the detective's help.

Ella hesitated, feeling that same unease ripple through her again. After Zimmerman's comment, could they really trust Chen to get this right? It seemed as if the chief didn't have a lot of faith in his detective.

But what other choice did they have?

Should they talk to the chief himself? No. That didn't feel right.

Then again, neither did talking to Chen. But why was that? Simply because Ella was suddenly suspicious of everyone? She wasn't suspicious of the detective, was she? Surely not.

"Here you are," a cheery waitress said as she appeared at their table. "I have two pink lemonades and two chicken salads with our raspberry vinaigrette dressing."

"Thank you," Ella said.

"Yeah, thanks," Jude echoed. When the waitress walked away, he smirked. "I've never eaten such a pink meal before."

Ella realized he was probably right. Pink lemonade. Pink dressing. Dark pink cranberries dotted over the salad.

"I don't think I've ever purposefully ordered a salad in my

life," he said, looking mildly put out. "I should've guessed your usual wasn't a bacon-filled club sandwich."

Ella smiled. "I'm sure the salad is delicious."

"Must be, if you order it every week." He reached for his fork but paused. "Ella, how are you doing financially?"

"What do you mean? Is this because I bought lunch?" she asked with a small laugh. Her smile slipped. "Oh. Are you worried about my loss of income now that the shop is destroyed?"

"Not just that," he said. "I'm wondering about before. You were taking some serious phone calls. You were on edge." He leaned forward, keeping his voice low to ensure no one else could hear. His words felt heavier now, sinking between them like stones. "Do you think you were in trouble with a loan shark? You always hear stories about how they go after people who can't pay."

Her eyebrows shot up. "I would never—" But she cut herself off. "I mean, I don't think I would." She glanced at her phone. "There's one way to find out." In moments, she'd logged into her bank account. She pulled up her most recent statement. Her balance wasn't overly impressive, but it was comfortable. A nest egg for a rainy day.

Or an emergency fund to cover her loss of income.

She continued to peruse her bank statements, going backward one month at a time. She finally glanced back at Jude. "I don't see anything out of the ordinary. I'm never in the red, not even when I go back to last fall. There's no deposit that looks unusual."

Jude absently munched on his salad, then nodded. "Okay. If you're sure. It was just a thought."

She took a sip of her lemonade, glancing around Rocky's again.

"You look troubled," Jude said.

"I'm sure it's nothing."

"What? What's nothing?"

"I've had the strangest feeling since we've been in here. I can't quite place it." She studied the faces of the people who were dining. Not one of them looked intimidating. But did that mean anything? Would she recognize the face of the man who wanted her dead? A dark pulse of dread beat through her chest, fast and sharp.

Jude glanced over his shoulder, studying the other patrons as well.

"It's probably nothing," Ella repeated. None of the patrons seemed to be paying any attention to her. Not even Chief Zimmerman and his small crew, who were now seated on the opposite side of the café digging into hearty sandwiches and fries. No one looked nefarious in any way. "Maybe it's just the memory of being in here with Madison."

That had to be it. Somehow, just thinking of her set Ella's nerves on edge.

"Maybe," Jude said, but the tight set of his jaw told her he didn't believe it. He raised his hand, flagging down their waitress. "I'm sorry for the inconvenience, but something came up. Could we get a couple of to-go boxes?"

"Certainly," she replied as she scampered off to retrieve them.

They quickly packed up their meals and headed outside.

It was Jude who noticed the piece of white paper wedged under his windshield wiper. He carefully slid it free. Ella leaned across him, silently reading it along with him.

Leave it alone or you'll both be dead.

The words were scrawled in thick, messy letters, as if the writer had been in a rush, or barely able to control their rage.

"Get in the truck," he commanded, even as his gaze scanned the street looking for trouble. His voice, usually so steady, was low and fierce, brooking no argument. He opened the passenger door and she jumped inside. Fear hit Ella, coursing over her like a tidal wave. When would this end?

Jude hurried around to his side and hopped in, still scanning the street. "We weren't inside long. Fifteen, maybe twenty minutes. The only time I had my back to my vehicle was when we were ordering." He shook his head. "So whoever put it here is probably long gone."

"Leave it alone or you'll both be dead," Ella repeated, her voice barely above a whisper. "What do you think that means? Do you really think they'll back off if we stop looking for answers?"

Jude scoffed. "Not a chance. They're not going to stop. And that means we can't, either."

She knew what he wasn't saying.

If they didn't find these people first, they wouldn't live long enough to even try.

"What are you doing?" Ella asked when he pulled over to the curb on a side street.

"Just making a plan," Jude said, grabbing his phone from the cupholder, but the weight of the note on the windshield stayed heavy in his gut.

He'd been watching the rearview mirror the whole time, looping the edges of town, where traffic was light. Testing. Checking.

The note wasn't an immediate threat.

But the message was a warning and a warning meant things were escalating. Worse, it proved to Jude that he was keeping an eye on Ella. Whoever *he* was. And even worse than that, Jude hadn't been paying enough attention to notice. Never mind that he didn't watch his vehicle while they were at the counter ordering. The fact that they must've been followed in the first place ate at him.

What unsettled him more than the words was the fact that whoever left it had gotten that close.

Close enough to touch the truck. Close enough to see them.

And he hadn't seen a thing.

He flexed his fingers against the steering wheel.

Outside, the wind swirled across the street, scattering brittle leaves along the cracked pavement, sending them spinning like little warnings.

The sky hung heavy and low, a bruised, restless gray, the kind of sky that made him pull his jacket tighter without even thinking.

He nabbed his phone again. "I'm going to see if I can find any information on Annette Ballenger. Starting with an address."

He pulled up a quick online search. Almost immediately, Allen Ballenger's address popped up.

"I found the man Marjorie mentioned. His wife's name isn't listed, but that's not unusual. According to this, he lives in Arcadia Court. We don't know for sure that Allen and Annette are a couple, but there's one way to find out."

The housing development was less than ten minutes away.

"I think we should check it out," Jude said. "Are you game? Are you feeling okay? It's been a rough few days. Maybe I should take you back to the ranch and—"

"No." Ella hesitated for only a moment before nodding. "Let's do it. I'll rest later. I promise. But I feel like time is ticking away."

A dark sedan, the same one he thought he noticed earlier,

three cars back now, was hanging back just enough to stay out of obvious view.

His gut tightened.

He took the next turn sharply, without signaling.

Ella braced herself, shooting him a questioning look, but she stayed silent.

Jude risked a glance at the mirror. There it was again, the sedan following, making the same sudden turn. It was far enough back that he couldn't make out the license plate. The driver was probably trying to be inconspicuous, but Jude was on high alert after finding the note on the windshield.

"Hold on," he muttered. He picked up speed, weaving onto an older service road lined by fallow fields and abandoned sheds.

The sedan hesitated at the intersection, then sped to follow.

Ella stiffened. "They're following us."

"Not for long." Jude's jaw flexed and they veered onto another narrow back road bordered by skeletal trees. He was trying to lose them without drawing more attention, but if it came to it…

By the time he emerged onto the next paved road, the sedan was nowhere in sight.

Ella gripped the dashboard, breathing hard, visibly shaken.

Jude didn't slow until they were several miles away, hidden again among normal traffic.

Still, he kept glancing in the rearview mirror, his whole body tense.

"Did you get the license plate?" Ella asked, though her tone didn't sound too hopeful.

"I didn't," Jude grumbled. "They were too far away." Too close for comfort, too far for gathering details.

When they reached Arcadia Court, it was easy enough to find the house. A simple home, set back deep on a private lot.

The property was crowded with trees. Once they turned in, they wouldn't be visible to anyone driving by. He hadn't spotted the sedan again, and it would've been easily noticed on the nearly deserted road.

"Let's go see if we've tracked down the right person," Jude said.

Moments later they stood on the cement front steps as Jude rang the doorbell.

A few seconds passed before a middle-aged woman appeared. She pulled the door open, a questioning look on her face.

The first thing Jude noticed: straight, dark hair.

She wasn't athletic.

More gaunt than anything.

Still, could this be the woman that Stacey had described?

"Can I help you with something?" she asked.

Jude took a protective half step in front of Ella. Subtle, but deliberate.

"Annette Ballenger?" he asked.

"Yes, I'm Annette." She furrowed her brow, her gaze shifting around Jude and landing on Ella. "Oh, hello. You're the young woman from the antique shop."

"Yes," Ella said, stepping around Jude, clearly not appreciating his interference. "We have a few questions for you."

"Is this about the coins? If it is, I'm afraid I found a buyer. One that didn't pay me much," she added quietly, "but they're gone all the same."

"Actually, I'm here to find out what you might know about the attacks on my friend," Jude said.

Annette's eyes widened. She took a startled step back.

Good.

He wanted her off balance.

"Excuse me?" she asked, glancing between them.

"It seems someone has it out for Ella." Jude kept his voice level, watching her closely. "I heard you might've threatened her."

"What? No." Annette shook her head and turned fully to Ella. "I admit, I was extremely rude. I lost my temper. I've felt bad about it ever since. I even thought about stopping by the shop to apologize, but honestly… I was embarrassed."

"Ella's assistant said you seemed desperate. Angry," Jude said.

"I was angry," Annette admitted.

"Angry enough to have someone go after Ella?" Jude persisted.

Annette looked horrified. "No. I admit I was out of line. I was dealing with a lot, and I took it out on her. My daughter, Gwen, she's had a rough few years. Lost her husband. Their son was diagnosed with autism. She's been drowning in bills, and we've been trying to help, but…"

Her voice trembled.

"She almost lost her home. I was desperate. I shouldn't have come into your shop that day. I was rude. I regret it." Her gaze darted to Ella. "I truly am sorry."

"You never returned to the antique shop?" Jude asked. "Never had a confrontation with Ella in the alley?"

Annette's brow furrowed. "No. Why would you ask that?"

He mentally sidestepped the question. No need to reveal Ella's memory loss.

"We're just trying to get to the bottom of a few things," Jude said.

"No," Annette repeated firmly. "I never went back. I was embarrassed enough as it was."

Ella shifted. “I appreciate the apology. I’ll keep Gwen and her son in my prayers.”

Annette’s eyes filled. She gave a tight smile. “Thank you. Days before she would have been evicted, her church took up a special offering. She’s back on her feet now, at least for the moment.” She hesitated. “I’ll keep you in my prayers too. I hope you find whoever’s causing you trouble.”

“Thank you,” Ella said softly.

They stepped off the porch.

Back inside the truck, Ella finally broke the silence.

“Do you believe her?”

“Yeah,” Jude said, watching the mirror again. “She didn’t know we were coming. Her story was too detailed, too raw to fake on the spot.”

“Besides,” Ella added, “since I was attacked by a man, it means she would’ve had to send someone after me. Over some coins? Doesn’t seem likely.”

“Exactly.”

He tapped the steering wheel absently, his mind racing. Maybe this had been a waste of time, but it was the only lead they’d had. It would’ve been silly not to follow it. What else did they have to go on? Very little.

“It was a man that attacked you,” he said. “I started to second-guess myself, but I’ve been going over the confrontation in your hospital room. It had to have been a man, judging by the build.” Not to mention the power of the punch Jude had taken to the jaw. “But a woman that Stacey overheard you arguing with.” He shook his head. “Madison doesn’t fit the description. She’s tall. Blond. Nothing like what Stacey described.”

Ella frowned. “Then who?”

“I don’t know yet.” Jude’s voice was grim. “But I’m starting to think the mystery woman is the key to all of this.”

Ella stared out the window, silent.

The trees with their brilliant display of autumn leaves blurred past in blazing golds, fiery oranges and deep reds that shimmered in the sunlight like sparks caught in the wind. Here and there, hay bales dotted the field, and distant mountains, dusted with early snow, loomed beneath the silvery gray sky.

"And just how do we find her?" she asked.

It was rhetorical. Still, Jude answered.

"I have no idea."

But he knew one thing with bone-deep certainty.

They were running out of time. The note on the windshield was a warning, while the sedan following them had been a clear threat that this was not over yet.

EIGHT

The log-sided ranch house creaked and groaned against the rising wind, as if it was protesting the change in seasons. Ella tightened the quilt around her shoulders and stared out the front window, her heart knocking against her ribs.

The sky was an ominous charcoal-gray, the clouds thick and low, spinning the last of autumn's brittle leaves across the pasture. She hadn't realized how isolated Jude's ranch was until now. Down a long gravel driveway, the pasture was surrounded by woods, with no neighbors in sight, nothing but empty fields and dense tree lines.

He'd purchased it a few years ago, confiding to her after they'd been dating a while that he thought it felt like the perfect place to raise a family. She had wholeheartedly agreed and had even been able to picture them raising their kiddos here.

But tonight, it felt a little too secluded.

Bandit sat perched on the back of the recliner near the door, his tail flicking, his single eye narrowed toward the window. His body was tense, coiled, as if he sensed something—or someone—lurking just beyond the walls.

He suddenly let out a low, guttural growl, the eerie sound vibrating in the tense stillness of the room. His ears flattened against his head and his gaze fixed on the darkness beyond the window.

Ella's skin prickled with unease.

Then she heard the hum of a vehicle as Jude strode into the room. He'd been making a few calls. Checking in with Blake and his supervisor to see if anything needed attention at work, while she *tried* to rest, as she'd promised she would.

He slid the curtain open and peered out the window. "It's Lexie."

Ella felt her heart rate slow a bit. A few moments later, light footsteps tapped up the staircase leading to the porch, then Jude opened the door. Lexie entered carrying a pizza box and a two-liter bottle of ginger ale tucked awkwardly under one arm.

"I brought dinner," she announced, her voice too bright, like she was trying too hard.

Ella offered a small smile, but her stomach twisted painfully. She couldn't tell if it was nerves, guilt, or the persistent nausea left over from the concussion.

Lexie set the food on the coffee table and rubbed her hands against her thighs. Her gaze flicked to Ella, assessing. Not unkind, but not exactly welcoming, either. Their friendship did not seem as if it would rebound anytime soon.

"How's the patient?" Lexie asked.

Ella shrugged, not wanting to admit that she was feeling worn-out from all of the investigating they'd been doing. Or maybe it was the attempts on her life that had left her feeling so weary.

"She's tired," Jude said. "But she's doing okay."

Lexie dug her fists into her hips. "Oh, you mean, other than being shot at?"

Jude winced. "You heard about that?"

"The whole town has heard about it."

Ella sank deeper into the couch, trying to make herself small, out of the way. She couldn't ignore the uncomfortable weight of Lexie's presence. She didn't seem openly hostile, as she had the first night. But if she had, Ella couldn't blame her.

After all, she'd once left Jude without a backward glance. Now, he was risking everything to keep her safe.

Ella tried to put herself in Lexie's shoes. She was pretty sure she'd behave the same way. Be protective and aloof.

A lump formed in her throat. She stared at her hands, picking at the loose threads on the quilt, wishing she could explain. Not just to them, but to herself, what had happened. She wished she could go back in time and correct this wrong. Because breaking off her engagement felt very wrong.

The pizza smell turned her stomach, but she reached for a slice, anyway, when Lexie handed her a piece on a paper plate, not wanting to seem ungrateful.

Jude asked Lexie about her day, and as the siblings chatted, Ella nibbled at her food.

Bandit stretched and yawned, then hopped to the floor. He began pacing in front of the door, a clear sign he wanted out. Though he'd been rescued from the cold, he still demanded his outside time. He liked to wander but never went far from the ranch. The cat let out an annoyed yowl as he stood at the door.

Jude rose from his seat.

"Are you sure it's okay for him to go out?" Ella asked.

Jude hesitated only a moment. "He'll be fine. You know how he gets, Ella. I'm pretty sure he was raised as an outdoor cat. If I don't let him out, he'll get restless and start climbing the curtains."

That was true and Ella knew it. She'd seen it herself.

Jude let the cat out. But then he flipped the lock closed

again. That should make her feel better, but it somehow set her already frazzled nerves on edge instead.

One of the horses whinnied out in the pasture, then another one answered. Ella used to love the sound of them calling to one another, but now she worried that something was distressing them.

No, she needed to stop letting her imagination run away with her sensible thoughts. Just because someone was trying to kill her, didn't mean that there was danger *everywhere.*

I'm safe here, she told herself as she willed her rattling heart to believe it.

"Maybe we should call Chen," she said quietly.

Jude's mouth tightened. "Why? I trust that she wants to solve this. I'm not so sure I trust how she's handling it."

Ella frowned. "She's done everything she can. She's the one who's been checking on us."

"Yeah," Jude said grimly. "And she's the one Chief Zimmerman went out of his way to undermine at Rocky's."

The memory of the chief's slick smile, his subtle jab about Chen, crept back into Ella's mind. *She's got good instincts, but instincts can't replace real experience and we both know her track record isn't the best.* She hadn't wanted to believe it then. She didn't want to believe it now. But doubt curled inside her.

"What are you two talking about?" Lexie asked.

Jude frowned. They hadn't mentioned to Lexie that Detective Chen was now working Ella's case. He quickly filled her in.

"You don't trust her?" Lexie asked.

"It's not that I don't trust *her*," Jude said. "It's that..."

"He doesn't trust that she'll do a good job," Ella said softly.

Lexie set her pizza on her plate. "Jude, it's been years.

You need to let go of your grudge. I understand, better than you seem to think, how hard it is to not know what happened to Dad. But I also think Detective Chen did everything she possibly could at the time. You *know* the crime scene was compromised."

Ella had heard this part of the story before. Somehow, two news crews had beat law enforcement to the Pinecrest Landing, a rural boat access. An anonymous tip had been called in, back in the era when payphones could still occasionally be found, before security cameras were on every building. The news crews had trampled the area, taking their camera shots and video. By the time the police arrived, their footprints and tire tracks were everywhere.

"Yeah," Jude said to Lexie. "I'm aware. You also know I think whoever called it in did it on purpose. They wanted the crime scene messed up."

"I didn't know that," Ella said, sitting up a little straighter. "I mean, yes, I knew that the crime scene was contaminated, but I didn't realize you suspect it was intentional."

Jude had never mentioned it, she was sure of that.

He shrugged, but the gesture was full of tension. "It's just a hunch. One more thing that was never proven."

She heard the words he didn't say out loud: *Thanks to Detective Chen.*

He pushed up from his seat. "I'm not all that hungry. I'm going to go out to do a perimeter check."

Ella opened her mouth to argue but Lexie gave a subtle shake of her head. It wasn't until after the front door closed that Lexie spoke again.

"He needs to feel useful and he's a trained officer," Lexie said. "As much as I don't love the idea of him out there, he knows what he's doing."

"I know you're right. I just worry about him."

Lexie blew out a sigh, loud and borderline obnoxious. "I don't get it, Ella. It seems like you still care about him. He still cares about you. I just don't get what happened between you two."

"I *do* care about him," Ella admitted. "Of course, I do." More than she should, considering she'd given back the ring.

"Just don't hurt him. That's all I ask," Lexie said, her voice almost pleading.

"I won't," Ella promised. "Jude's helping me, but you don't have to worry. He's over me."

"And you're over him?" Lexie asked with an arched eyebrow.

"I'm sure you've had a really long day," Ella said, clumsily trying to dodge the question. "Thank you for bringing home the pizza. Why don't you go relax and I'll clean up?"

"*You* are supposed to be relaxing," Lexie said.

"That's not going to happen," Ella replied. "I need to stay busy. It won't take me long."

"Suit yourself," Lexie said. She grabbed the last corner of her pizza off her plate and trudged up the staircase.

Ella stood and gathered their plates. She tossed them in the trash, then washed her hands in the sink and glanced out the window. The horses looked peaceful now, grazing in the field, in the hazy twilight. Bandit was nowhere to be seen, probably searching for mice in the barn. And Jude? Ella couldn't see him, but she knew he was out there, keeping watch, keeping her safe.

She couldn't help but think of all that Jude's family had been through. Their mother, Denise had left Haven Creek months after Lexie had graduated from high school. She had told her children she just couldn't bear to live in the town where her husband had been killed. She'd moved to Utah and had since remarried. She visited every few months, though, and she and Ella had always gotten along well. But Ella knew that Jude missed having his mom nearby. It was another deep loss to him.

She could remember the deep love they'd shared and knew that their breakup would have been another emotional blow. She hated thinking she had caused him hurt.

Her heart stirred. She ached over what she couldn't remember, and wondered if there was any way to fix what was now so broken between them. She couldn't think about that now. It wouldn't be fair to herself, to Jude, or even to Lexie. The pull toward him was growing harder to ignore. But no matter how much she wanted to lean into it, she couldn't. Not after everything. Not when she'd made a promise she intended to keep.

Jude shot up in bed, straining his eyes to see in the dark, his heart hammering as he tried to make sense of what awakened him.

Had it been a nightmare? Sleep had eluded him for hours as he replayed the events of the past few days.

He'd awakened with a start a few times already as horrible images of Ella hurt, and worse, flooded his mind.

This time felt different, though. He heard frantic whinnies coming from the pasture. Was there a wolf? A cougar? Rare, but not impossible. He'd dealt with both in his work as a game warden. A cacophony of sounds erupted simultaneously from the porch, which rested directly below his bedroom window.

The violent, relentless growl of Bandit.

The loud bang and rattle that could only be the wrought-iron furniture tipping over.

Muttered curse words. Male. Definitely not Ella or Lexie. Definitely *not* a wolf or cougar.

Before his mind even had time to wrap around what he was hearing, he'd grabbed his firearm off the nightstand and was racing down the hallway to the staircase.

"What is it? What's going on?" Lexie's frantic voice reached him as she opened the door to the spare bedroom.

"Call nine-one-one," he commanded as he charged down the staircase.

"I'm doing that now," Ella said as she emerged from his den, holding her phone.

The thudding and banging ended as he flew past Ella. Jude flipped on the porchlight. The glow caught a man sprinting down the driveway.

He tossed open the door and raced after him, barely aware of Ella's cry for him to be careful.

Gravel bit at his bare feet but he paid it no heed.

Clementine and Ramona stampeded toward the far fence. He could hear their hooves pounding the hard ground as they let out shrill whinnies of distress. The other three horses trotted after them, also making their displeasure known. He noted their direction and behavior automatically, thanks to instincts honed from years of tracking wildlife and reading animal signs in the field.

The man was nearly lost in the darkness, but Jude managed to keep sight of his silhouette.

Moonlight shone down through patchy clouds.

His long gravel driveway snaked out before them, a pale contrast to the dark grass.

"Stop!" he commanded, not at all surprised when the man didn't comply. "I'll shoot!" he shouted.

His words seemed to spur the man into running even faster.

He knew if he stopped, if he took aim, if he fired, he would be able to hit the guy. Despite all this man had done—

shooting at Ella, invading her home, damaging her shop, coming here tonight—he couldn't, wouldn't, shoot a man in the back.

That's the way his father had died.

And even with his extensive firearm training as a state game warden, he still hesitated. It wasn't just about hitting a target. It was about what came after. Instead, he fired as he ran, knowing full well that his shot would go wide.

The shot split the night air, sharp and unforgiving, echoing through the pasture, upsetting the horses all over again.

The man didn't stop—he only ran faster, tearing down the driveway like a hunted animal.

"Consider that a warning shot!" he bellowed. The intruder raced out onto the road. "If you come back," Jude shouted as he reached the end of the driveway, "next time I won't miss!"

He reached the mailbox in time to see the runner yank open the door of a waiting car.

A black sedan? It was impossible to tell in the dark.

The dome light did not flash on as he hopped inside.

The car tore off, tires tearing up the gravel as they raced away.

The moonlight didn't cast enough of a glow for him to see much. The shape of the vehicle, definitely a car, not an SUV or a truck, was all he could ascertain. It was a dark blob as it headed north, the opposite direction from town, where the police would be coming from.

He watched as the car continued to barrel away from him, dust flying up, hovering over the road like fog floating over the pasture on a misty morning.

His heart thundered painfully. They had planned this. One driver, one man on foot. Coordinated. Calculated. And now, it confirmed something he hadn't been sure of before. The man in the hospital wasn't working alone.

There were at least two people involved in this.

Was one the dark-haired woman from the alleyway?

He punched a hand through the air in frustration, letting out a guttural growl. Maybe he should've shot the guy. He had tried to kill Ella.

Frustration sizzled through him. What if this had been his only chance to save her?

What if these people just kept coming back?

Jude thought they probably would.

And he'd missed his opportunity.

He pivoted, his bare feet plodding along the cool gravel driveway as his mind replayed events. If given the choice to do things over again, he was sure he couldn't have shot the guy. Shooting someone was traumatic enough, but shooting a guy in the back? He didn't think he'd have been able to live with himself if he'd done that.

But the tight ball of helpless frustration in his chest didn't care much for principles right now. It wanted justice. Most of all, right now, he wanted answers.

He would go back to his house and continue to do his best to keep Ella safe.

He would continue to pray, because he knew that God could turn this situation around in a heartbeat.

Anxious to get back to the house, he broke into a jog. He spotted Bandit by the railing, basking in the glow of the porchlight.

The cat sat on his haunches, languorously licking his paw and then stroking himself behind the ear, as if supremely pleased with himself for a job well done. Jude realized then what must have happened. Bandit liked to sleep in the rafters. Bandit did *no*t like strangers. He was certain that the cat had jumped down and attacked the man in the darkness, causing the utter chaos.

As he drew near, he spotted something else.

Ella stepped outside, a tentative look on her face before he had time to inspect his find.

"We heard gunshots," she began. "Did you...? Is he...?" Her words faded off.

"It was a warning shot," Jude said. "They got away."

"They?" Ella asked.

Jude grimaced. "The man who came up to the house, and ran, well, he had a driver. A getaway car. And before you ask, no, I wasn't able to make out either person. The only reason I know it was a man who was up here, by the house, was because I heard the timbre of his voice through the window when Bandit attacked him."

"You're okay?" Her gaze roamed over him and he nodded.

He could see her shoulders relax, the tension visibly fading away.

Lexie poked her head out onto the porch. "All clear?"

"All clear," Jude confirmed.

Jude stopped before he reached the steps.

Ella's eyes popped and she pointed at something in the shadows. "What's that?"

"A five-gallon gas can," he muttered. It had tipped over on its side, the gas sloshing out onto the gravel drive, making a muddy mess.

"That's what I thought," Ella said. Her voice shook and he knew realization had hit her as well.

Jude's stomach lurched because the intruder's purpose suddenly became all too clear.

He'd intended to douse the house in gasoline, or maybe just the doors and windows to hinder their escape. He climbed the steps and gave Bandit an affectionate, thankful pat.

Had the intruder really intended to burn Jude's home to the ground with everyone inside?

Yes, he realized, that was most likely the plan.

He turned to Ella and found himself looking into her wide, terrified eyes.

"It's okay," he said, though he knew it really wasn't.

If Bandit hadn't attacked, alerting them to the presence of the intruder, their situation would be very different right now. He scooped up the animal, and Bandit, for once, didn't protest.

They wouldn't now be standing on the porch waiting for law enforcement.

They'd likely be sleeping, unaware that flames were engulfing the outside, ready to burn them alive.

Ella shuddered.

Reflexively, he pulled her into his arms. Careful of the purring cat clutched between them, Ella sagged against his chest, the realization of what had almost occurred a heavy burden to bear.

"I hate to break up the cuddles," Lexie said in a voice that said she truly didn't, "but help has arrived."

Jude shot her a frustrated look, even as Ella stepped out of his arms.

A patrol car tore down the driveway, bouncing to a stop in front of them.

Blake got out, looked around and asked, "What happened?"

They stepped inside the house, where Jude gave him a rundown of events.

"I'll bring the gas can in, see if our techs can lift prints off it," Blake said. "But it's doubtful. The texture of the plastic will make it extremely difficult. I can request surveillance footage for the neighboring gas stations, see if we can catch our guy filling up."

"That's a long shot, too, isn't it," Ella said, not really asking a question.

"It is," Blake admitted. "The gas can itself looks old. It's faded and covered in dust, so trying to narrow down a purchase of the actual can is a moot point. Unfortunately, because it is old, the gas in it could be old as well. Still, it's worth looking into. Sometimes criminals do dumb things. Hopefully we'll get a break in the case soon."

"Apparently I've been getting phone calls precisely at noon every Wednesday," Ella said. "The number is blocked but I let Detective Chen know. She's going to look into it."

"For all the good that'll do," Jude muttered.

"Hey," Blake said, "I know you have your reasons for doubting Detective Chen's abilities, but I assure you, she's good at what she does. Unfortunately, the calls could be tied to a burner phone and then there won't be much she can do." He leveled a look at Jude. "And that won't be her fault."

"And in the meantime?" Lexie demanded. "We just wait for them to come after us again."

"They're not after you," Jude reminded her. "Maybe it's time you went home. You'd be safer there. Or better yet, take a vacation. Go stay with Mom and Henry. I'd feel better if you were two states away."

She crossed her arms over her chest and lifted her chin in her usual defiant way. "Not a chance. I'm not bailing just because things are heated. Besides, I can't afford to take time off work right now. I don't have enough leave built up and I can't just take time off without pay. I have a costly furnace repair to pay for."

Jude knew it was more than the furnace. As much as he'd like his sister out of harm's way, he knew she wanted to stay for moral support. She was stubborn and arguing with her would be futile.

"Given the circumstances," Blake said, "I'm going to stand watch the rest of the night. We've had officers doing drive-bys, but that's clearly not enough. Then I'm going to put in a request to do the same the next few nights while I'm on duty. After that, I have a few days off. Hopefully we've caught these guys by then, but if not, I'll stand guard on my own time."

He motioned toward the front door.

"You all might as well try to get some sleep. I doubt they'll be back tonight, but if they are, I'll be waiting."

"Thanks, Blake," Jude said. He appreciated his friend's vigilance but he didn't think any of them would be sleeping well.

Not tonight.

Not until this was over. Not until whoever wanted Ella dead was behind bars…or buried six feet under.

NINE

Ella tried to discreetly take calming breaths—in through her nose, out through her mouth—as the insurance adjuster took pictures and made notes as he walked through her shop. They had finally received clearance from the police department to enter the building. This was the first time she'd seen inside, and the damage was devastating.

The air smelled of smoke and burnt wood, a sharp reminder of everything she had lost. She refused to cry, though the tears were threatening. Jude had held out his arms to her once, a silent offer of comfort, and she had pretended not to notice. She was trying to honor Lexie's request, but she wondered if her friend knew just how hard that was. Falling into Jude's arms was second nature to her. Every instinct screamed for her to let him in. She needed the comfort she knew he could provide, but she reminded herself she had no business taking it from him.

She swiped a finger under her eye, quickly wiping away a tear before it could escape. Items that weren't physically damaged were covered in a sheet of soot from the fire. Everything would need to be meticulously, painstakingly cleaned—item by item. So many things.

In through her nose, out through her mouth. How could she ever pick up the pieces? So much damage done. In through her nose, out through her mouth. Deep calming breaths.

Please, Lord, give me strength.

Jude clasped her elbow, pulling her aside. "How are you doing?"

She shook her head, not trusting her voice to speak. Her life was in ruins. What was she supposed to say? How could she even begin to start over? Ella's Attic wasn't like other businesses, where she could just go online and order more inventory. Every piece was unique, either purchased by Ella at flea markets and estate sales, or brought to her by someone who saw its value.

"I think I'm done here," Tyler Hancock, the insurance adjuster, said. "I'll go over everything and be in touch."

Ella thanked him, though her voice was strained, and she watched him walk out the door.

For a long moment, she and Jude stood there, surrounded by her smoke-stained memories and blackened hopes.

"It's okay. Everything is going to be okay," she murmured, more for her own benefit than Jude's. It didn't feel okay. She knew she had to concentrate on what was important. "Nobody was hurt. These are just things. Things that can be replaced."

Well, not really. They were antiques and some had been one-of-a-kind items. Her heart sank, but she couldn't dwell on the loss.

"You'll have the store up and running before you know it," Jude assured her.

She appreciated his confidence but didn't feel the same. As she glanced around, all she felt was a desire to run out the door and keep on running. It would be so easy to leave Haven Creek. Take the payout from the insurance and cut her losses. But she didn't want to leave. Not really.

It would be so easy to pack up and go back to Helena, spend more time with her parents. But something was holding her back.

She didn't want to admit that the *something* was Jude. But it was. Despite the promise she had made to Lexie, she couldn't shake the growing feelings she had for the man she had once loved. And honestly, deep down, still did, despite the lingering confusion and doubt she felt.

Lord, I don't even know where I'm supposed to be anymore. Show me. Guide me. Please don't let me run away from something You meant me to face.

"We should get going," Jude said. He had been keeping watch, almost obsessively, Ella had noticed, as she met with the adjuster, but he was clearly anxious to get out of here before trouble struck again. "There isn't anything we can do here."

She knew what he really meant. He wanted to get her back to the ranch, where he felt she was safer. If he'd had his way, she wouldn't have met with the insurance adjuster today. He'd stated it was too dangerous, but she felt she needed to, so he'd begrudgingly agreed to take her into town. Now, he was anxious to get her back home.

Jude hustled her across the street.

"I hope Mr. Hancock moves quickly," Ella said. "I'm anxious to get my life back in order. I should call Marjorie to let her know I met with the adjuster. I'm sure she'd like the update. I'm so relieved that she's working during her retirement because she wants to and not because she needs the money." That, at least, left Ella one less thing to worry about.

When it became clear that Jude had not heard a word she said, she gave his shoulder a nudge. "Jude?"

She swung her gaze down the street to determine what held his attention in its grip.

"Isn't that Madison?" he asked.

Once he mentioned it, Ella spotted the young woman immediately. Her long blond hair was curled to perfection. She wore a yellow sundress, denim jacket and chunky heels. She did not look as if she'd just come from roughing it, camping somewhere out of cell-phone range.

Ella's heart slammed against her ribs, as if in warning, but she couldn't stop herself from shouting out to the woman who was supposedly her friend.

"Madison!" Ella called, the name leaving her mouth almost reflexively.

Madison's gaze darted her way. She froze, and Ella had the oddest feeling she was debating bolting.

There was something about the way Madison looked at her. Ella was sure she'd seen a moment of panic, a flicker of something she couldn't place, that made her pulse quicken and sent a sizzle of fear for her friend spiraling through her.

After a moment, she gave a small wave, smiled and then pivoted nonchalantly, as if she'd forgotten something. She took off in the opposite direction, not exactly hustling down the sidewalk, but at a much quicker pace than a leisurely stroll.

Jude and Ella exchanged a perplexed look, then, in silent agreement, they took off after Madison.

She didn't hurry her steps as they approached, but Ella was sure she could see the woman's shoulders tensing. She was surely well aware of Jude and Ella's hurried footsteps catching up to her.

"Madison!" Ella called again as she and Jude closed the distance between them.

Madison stopped. Hesitated. Then spun around.

A huge, and so very fake-looking smile adorned her face.

"Hey, Ella, it's good to see you," she said in a tone that implied it wasn't good at all.

"Really?" Ella tried to keep her tone light. *Because it looked to me like you couldn't get away from us fast enough.*

Madison's gaze darted around the street. Her plastered-on smile slipped.

Ella stiffened slightly, feeling as if unseen eyes were crawling over her skin. Watching. Waiting. Oh, was she ever going to get over this paranoia?

"Look, I'm sorry I haven't called you yet. I just got back. This morning. I just got back this morning," she said, nodding as if to convince herself as well as Ella and Jude. "I've been busy running errands for Mom. You remember she's sick, right?"

"Yes, of course," Ella said, her tone gentling. She remembered *that*, even if she didn't remember the last few months.

Madison had been one of the people she'd spent those missing months with, but all Ella had was fragments of information. All of it supplied by other people. The information didn't add up to much. Had she and Madison really become close? The woman wasn't acting as if they'd been good friends.

"I don't mean to keep you, but I'd really like to talk to you. It's important," Ella said, keeping her voice low, but firm.

Madison's gaze continued to bounce around, making Ella paranoid. Was the young woman afraid they were being watched?

If so, by whom? Did that mean she knew something? Or was Ella reading too much into the woman's behavior?

"I'm kind of in a hurry," Madison said, her mouth set into a firm line, all traces of her smile gone.

"Did you have a nice camping trip?" Jude asked, ignoring her claim.

"Oh, yes. It was fine," Madison said with another nod.

"Where did you go?" Jude persisted.

Madison frowned. "It was a small campground. A few hours from here. On a small lake. I'm sure you've never heard of it." She winced, almost imperceptibly, and Ella wondered if the woman had remembered too late that Jude was a game warden and was probably well aware of every body of water in the state.

"Even better," Jude said lightly as he flashed her a charming smile. "Camping is sort of a hobby of mine. I'm always looking for new places to try. So what was this campground called?"

She shrugged, her mouth opening and closing a few times before she finally forced words out.

"I don't recall. My friends made the reservations. It was just across the border, into Wyoming," She laughed a brittle, uncomfortable-sounding laugh. "All I had to do was show up."

She took a step away from them.

"What was the lake called?" Jude asked, his tone curious and easy.

She looked everywhere but at Jude.

"I don't know. I don't think my friends mentioned the name. Look, I can't talk right now."

"Why not?" Jude asked.

Her eyes darted to him and she took a step back.

"I—I need to get home to Mom. She needs her medicine." She lifted a small white paper bag into the air. It was printed with the name of the pharmacy just down the block.

If Ella wasn't mistaken, the bag trembled slightly in Madison's grip. Clearly, whatever else the young woman was up to, taking care of her mother really was a top priority.

"I'm sorry," she said, her tone tight. "But I really do need to go."

"Can I call you later?" Ella asked. "Or better yet, can we meet up?"

Madison shook her head firmly. "I don't think so. I can't help you."

"You don't even know what I want to talk to you about," Ella said. *Or do you?*

"I'm sorry, Ella. Really sorry," Madison said. The earnestness of her tone suggested to Ella that she was apologizing for something far more complicated than not being able to stick around to chat.

Her gaze flitted around, then she darted past them and took off again. Her clunky sandals slapped against the sidewalk with each hurried step.

"I feel like we should go after her," Jude said.

"I don't think it would do any good," Ella replied.

"You're right. But she's scared. I feel like every other sentence out of her mouth was a lie. Something is up with her. She's hiding something. Something big. I can feel it."

Ella nodded her agreement. "I know. She never went camping. That's pretty obvious."

She watched Madison's retreating form with a knot of dread twisting in her stomach.

Along with not knowing a thing about the supposed campground, Madison looked far too put-together to have just come from roughing it this morning. Her makeup was flawless, her nails recently manicured, her eyebrows neatly plucked. Her hair had been curled into flowing waves.

They watched as Madison hopped into her shiny red SUV and peeled away.

"She's the police chief's daughter," Jude said, mirroring Ella's thoughts. "What could she possibly have to be so afraid of?"

"And why is she determined to get away from me?" Ella asked. "I thought we were friends."

Though she was taking Joanne's word for it.

Maybe Joanne was wrong. Had the woman unknowingly misled her? Maybe Ella and Madison hadn't really gotten together after every Bible study. Maybe she barely knew the young lady at all.

She voiced her thoughts to Jude.

"Maybe Joanne is mistaken."

He frowned. "I don't think so. The waitress at Rocky's confirmed you were there often. If not with Madison, who? Madison is spooked, but she wasn't acting like you two weren't friends. She's running scared, and judging by the way she was looking around, she's nervous to be seen with you. Why?"

"I wish I knew," Ella murmured.

But deep down, she was starting to fear the truth.

Whatever Madison knew…it was dangerous.

"Let's get out of here," Jude said, his voice low and tight. Madison was clearly rattled, and that set his own nerves on edge. What, or whom, had she been looking for? She knew more than she was letting on. Of that, he was certain.

"Maybe we should stop by her house," he suggested, even as his gut churned. "She might be willing to talk there. She mentioned she needed to get home to her mom, so it sounds like she still lives there."

"She was carrying a pharmacy bag. I do remember that Madison is a nursing student, or has she received her degree by now?" Ella murmured. "Regardless, I think she lives with her mom to help care for her."

Before they'd gone more than a few feet, something snagged Jude's attention. Like Madison had done, he began to scan the street, looking for anything out of place. The man who suddenly poked his head around the corner down the block, gun raised, was most definitely out of place.

His hood was up, aviators shielding much of his face. Cold adrenaline slammed through Jude's veins.

"Shooter!" he barked, simultaneously tackling Ella. They hit the ground hard as a shot cracked the air.

He half lugged, half rolled Ella off the curb, using a maroon minivan for cover. Another shot rang out and the minivan's windshield shattered, glass shards raining down.

Screams ripped through the air as panic fractured the street. A young mother hoisted her two children with superhuman strength and dove into a bakery. Others bolted into storefronts, some tripping in their terror. Cars screeched and fishtailed as they peeled out of parking spots, desperate to flee.

Jude reached for his weapon. No way in the world was he just going to sit here and cower. Crouching, he edged around the minivan.

The shooter crept toward them, gun steady, steps deliberate.

Jude quickly scanned nearby windows and rooftops, his instincts screaming that one shooter might not be the only threat. A flash of movement caught his eye in an upstairs window across the street. But it was just someone ducking for cover. His pulse jackhammered in his ears, but he shoved the distraction aside, locking his focus on the man advancing.

Now that people had ducked for cover, Jude didn't hesitate. He squeezed off a shot. The cement near the gunman's feet exploded in a spray of dust and rock. The man let out a bark of outrage and dove behind a silver Mercedes.

As far as serious situations went, Jude couldn't think of one he hated more. Madman, loaded weapon, innocent civilians. It was a recipe for disaster.

Staying low, he peered through the cracked, lightly tinted window of the minivan. From this new angle, he spotted the gunman bolting across the street. He disappeared down the sidewalk, moving fast.

Jude itched to give chase. But what if he wasn't alone? What if the dark-haired woman was still lurking? Or whoever his accomplice, his getaway driver, had been? He wasn't about to leave Ella unprotected. Besides, one wrong move could turn this into a real mess.

Ella was his priority. Always.

A fresh surge of worry lanced through him. She was still recovering from a concussion, still bruised and hurting. Another fall like that and he didn't want to think about the damage it could do. She needed rest. Not more danger. And he had failed again to keep her out of harm's way.

He scanned the area again. Nothing obvious, no new threats.

"Come on," he said, hauling Ella to her feet. He used his body to shield her as best he could as they hurried along the vehicles, his gun raised, eyes constantly scanning.

His truck was close. After unlocking it with a quick click, he shoved the door open and practically tossed Ella inside.

Sirens howled somewhere nearby. Vehicles edged cautiously back onto the road. Were they civilians…or something worse?

"Stay down," he ordered.

Jude sprinted around to the driver's side, jumped in, gunned the engine and peeled away from the chaos, careful not to draw attention, but fast enough to make it clear they weren't sticking around.

At the edge of town, Jude let himself breathe.

"No sign of him?" Ella asked, unfolding herself cautiously.

"No."

"I texted Detective Chen while we were behind the van. Faster than calling. She told us to stay put," Ella said grimly. "I said it was too late. We were already gone."

Jude grunted but shook his head. "I don't want to talk to Chen. Or Chief Zimmerman. Not right now."

Ella frowned, concern tightening her features. "Jude, Chen is trying to help."

He glanced over, his jaw tight. "You say that, but what has she actually done?"

"Probably a whole lot, we just don't know about it," Ella insisted, voice rising a notch. "We can't expect answers overnight. I trust her heart in this."

The truck rumbled over a pothole, and neither spoke for a long moment, tension crackling in the cab between them.

Jude dragged a hand through his hair. "I don't like this. He's getting reckless. And reckless people make mistakes. Hopefully enough to get himself caught."

Or someone else is going to get killed first. The thought knifed into Jude's mind and stayed there, jagged and cold.

The thought of Ella, dead. He could barely stand it.

He was trying so hard to keep his feelings for her at bay, but he was fighting a losing battle and he knew it.

This had to end. Soon.

And he was convinced Madison knew exactly what was going on.

She was scared. She'd expected something today. Had someone been following her, too?

Would she talk now? If they caught her off guard? Or managed to track her down somewhere private?

"Where are we going?" Ella asked when he veered off the expected turn to the ranch.

Jude's eyes kept flicking to the rearview mirror.

"I think we need to catch up with Madison," he said. "She knew we were being watched, or at least suspected it. If she knows that, she must know who's after you. Either that or you're both being watched."

"I don't think she's going to be very willing to talk."

"I'm hoping if we catch her at home, where she feels safe…" He trailed off, uncertain.

If not, he had no problem letting Detective Chen hammer the truth out of her.

A dark SUV appeared briefly in his rearview mirror. His shoulders tensed.

He made an unnecessary right turn onto a residential side street. The SUV didn't follow. But the tension gripping his spine didn't ease. Had the SUV been a real threat? Or was he just going to see trouble everywhere until this ordeal came to an end?

He double-checked the address in his mind. The chief's house wasn't hard to find. The Zimmermans were a prominent family. Someone, somewhere along the way, had pointed it out to Jude at one time.

As he turned into the circular driveway, a new tension twisted in his gut.

No cars outside.

Maybe Madison had parked in the garage. Maybe.

He got out first, scanning their surroundings with a warden's instinct before walking Ella to the door.

The bell gonged inside the house like a warning as they stood on the covered porch. Jude had edged just slightly behind Ella, keeping her shielded from the road as best as he could.

The door opened a moment later. A casually dressed woman greeted them, her posture guarded.

"Hello," Ella said, her tone light, pleasant. "My name is Ella Clarke. I'm a friend of Madison's."

"Oh, hello," the woman said, "I'm Colleen. I help out with Vivian, Madison's mother, while the chief's at work. Madison left about an hour ago. She's not back yet."

Ella and Jude exchanged grim glances.

"You could try calling her," Colleen offered.

"I did," Ella said smoothly. Never mind that it had been the day before. "I wasn't able to reach her. I heard she was at a campground this week and didn't have reception."

"Campground?" Colleen laughed. "Madison wouldn't survive a night outdoors. A picnic is too much for her. She—"

Noticing the grim look on her visitors' faces, she cut herself off, as if realizing she may have admitted to something she shouldn't have.

Colleen's smile faltered. "Then again, what do I know?"

"Was Madison home this week?" Jude asked.

Colleen bit her lip, hesitating. "I really can't say."

"Can't or won't?" Jude leaned forward slightly.

"Shouldn't," Colleen clarified, her tone sharpening. "If you need something from Madison, talk to Madison."

"That's what we're trying to do," Ella said, her tone gentle. "We're worried about her."

Behind Colleen, a frail figure shuffled into view.

"Madison? Is something wrong with my Madison?" Vivian's weak voice cracked.

Colleen flinched. She moved fast, putting a protective hand on Vivian's shoulder. "No, dear. Nothing to worry about."

"I thought I heard her name." Vivian's brow wrinkled in confusion, her gaze narrowed on Ella, as if trying to focus.

"Oh, it's you. You have what you need. You'll make everything alright."

Jude's heart skipped a beat. What did that mean? It was almost as if the words had been said with an edge of relief, maybe even expectation, and his gut tightened. "Vivian—"

"Let's go inside," Colleen interrupted smoothly, as she gently tugged at the older woman's arm. "I'll fix us a snack."

Jude felt a pang of sympathy as he caught Vivian's lost, worried expression. Had there been a moment of clarity? Or had he just imagined it? Had the woman's words meant something? Or had they just been confused murmurings?

He shared a quick glance with Ella and saw the same questions flicker in her eyes.

Vivian studied Ella a moment longer, and she looked flustered all over again. "Do I know you?"

Ella smiled brightly. "Just a friend of Madison's."

Vivian nodded vaguely, her mind already fading into confusion.

"If I see Madison," Colleen said as she ushered Vivian back inside, "I'll pass along the message that you're looking for her."

Then the door shut firmly in their faces.

Jude let out a sharp exhale. "Well, that was a waste."

"Not completely," Ella said. "Now we know for a fact Madison lied about the campground."

And no one lied unless they had something to hide.

TEN

"Is it just me," Ella asked as Jude hustled her to his truck, "or was that comment odd?"

"Vivian murmuring that you'll make everything alright?" Jude asked. "That comment? Yeah. I thought it was a bit strange. But then again, she might've thought you were someone else. Or maybe her time frame is off. She could be remembering something in the past, confusing you with another person. In her condition, it's hard to say."

"She also said I have everything I need." Ella's brow furrowed. "Do you think she mistook me for someone else?"

"Maybe you do have something," Jude said. "The intruder at your house sure seemed to be looking for something."

"True." Her frown deepened.

He could tell how hard she was struggling to remember.

"Do you think Colleen was hiding something?" Ella asked. "She seemed intent on getting Vivian away from us."

Jude thought about that a moment as he opened the passenger door for Ella. He was tempted to hoist her inside, but now that she had recovered a bit, he thought she probably wouldn't appreciate his help. "No, actually, I got the impression she was just being protective. It's her job to care for Vivian."

He closed her door and jogged around to the driver's side. When he glanced up, he saw that Vivian was watching from the picture window. She raised her hand in a small wave. He waved back reflexively. She let the curtain fall and stepped away from the window.

Ella glanced at her phone as they pulled out of the driveway. "I missed a call from Detective Chen," she said. She winced as she listened to the voice mail. "She's checking out things downtown, then headed to the ranch and wants to meet us there."

Jude felt a twinge of annoyance that he knew he shouldn't feel. It was the detective's job to stay on top of things, and, of course, she would want to question them about the shooting. They probably should've made it a point to connect with Chen immediately—more than just the text Ella had sent. But his first thought was to get Ella to safety, and the second was to try to connect with Madison as quickly as possible.

Where had she gone after tearing off in her vehicle? Surely, she wasn't involved in the shooting. Was she? He felt as though he didn't know anything anymore.

"You can let Chen know we're headed back there now," he said.

When Ella said nothing, he glanced at her. She was staring straight ahead, a contemplative expression on her face.

"You okay?"

She nodded slowly. "I just thought of something. Can we stop by my house?"

He flicked a surprised glance her way, even as he turned his blinker on to loop back that way. "You remembered something?"

"Yes." She paused. "Kind of. Not anything from the last few months, but something else."

"What?" he asked, his curiosity piqued.

"The way my house was torn apart indicates that the intruder was looking for something. You just said so."

"It would seem logical."

"Something I must have," she muttered, almost to herself.

"So it would seem." He ground out a sound of frustration. "No matter how I spin it in my mind, I can't imagine what these people are looking for, how it could be tied to Madison and who this dark-haired lady could be."

"Maybe the dark-haired lady has nothing to do with this," Ella said. She didn't sound very convinced. He just let her comment slide.

"Please tell me you remember what they're looking for," he said.

She scoffed. "No. Not exactly. But if there's something at my house, I might know where I put it," she said, her tone cautious. "I know we should head to the ranch, Chen will be there soon, but could we check my place out quick?"

"Absolutely." If there was even the slightest chance of finding a clue, at this point, they needed to take it.

Within minutes they were in front of Ella's house. Jude scanned the street to be sure they hadn't been followed. He only hoped that whoever was after Ella wasn't staking her place out. He didn't see anyone he deemed suspicious.

"Hang tight," he said. He hopped out of the truck and hustled around to her side. He opened the door for her, then kept Ella in front of him with his body between her and the street.

She had her key out and stuck it in the front door as soon as they reached it. The door swung open, and they hurried inside. He locked the door behind him, even as Ella bustled toward the kitchen.

By the time he reached her, she was standing on a kitchen chair, reaching for the cabinet over the refrigerator.

He quirked an eyebrow. "That's your supersecret hiding place?"

She gave him a wry look. "Let's hope so." She opened the cabinet and pulled out a cookie jar, one he'd never seen before.

"This was my grandmother's. I never use it, but can't bear to part with it," she explained. She cradled the jar in her hands as Jude grabbed her elbow and guided her off the chair. She was still recovering from a head injury. He didn't want her risking another fall. One hit to the head had already been too much.

"Unbelievable," Jude muttered under his breath. Ella either didn't hear him, or chose to ignore him. He thought it was probably the latter. The cookie jar was shaped like a gingerbread house. It was large, gaudily painted. It was a bit on the hideous side. No wonder she kept it tucked out of sight. But this was where she kept things of value?

She placed it on the countertop and carefully lifted off the roof.

"Find anything?"

"I'm not sure." Ella peered inside. "I don't remember putting this here. The last thing I remember hiding was an antique wedding set I forgot to drop off at the jewelers to have a prong replaced. It was worth a small fortune. Another time, I didn't make it to the bank before closing. I didn't want to put that much cash in the drop box, so I brought it home with me." She shrugged. "I should probably invest in a safe, but I haven't yet. I've just used this."

Jude glanced at the window, half-expecting a pipe bomb to come sailing through.

His fingers tapped an impatient rhythm against the countertop.

"This doesn't look promising," Ella murmured.

A manila envelope had been rolled up and stuffed inside.

She reached in and pulled it out. It was flat. Maybe documents of some kind?

She opened the utensil drawer and grabbed a butter knife.

Jude clenched his fists at his sides, resisting the urge to

grab the envelope and tear it open himself. Every second felt drawn-out, weighted with urgency. He didn't like being here, where his truck was easily spotted from the driveway.

Ella slid the dull blade under the flap and carefully slit it open, clearly trying not to damage whatever was inside. She set down the knife and slowly pulled the contents free.

Jude's pulse ticked faster. He wanted to see. *Needed* to see. Was this finally the key to understanding why someone had targeted her?

Before he had a chance to do so, Ella skimmed the page of what looked like an old newspaper clipping. The paper was yellowed and looked brittle. She gasped, her face turning white.

The blood drained from her face so fast, Jude instinctively reached out, afraid she might faint.

"What is it?" he demanded. He reached for the items, but she took a step back. "Ella? You have to let me see."

She glanced up at him, confusion in her eyes. "I don't know what I expected. But it wasn't this. It's about your dad."

"My dad?" Disbelief colored his tone. He snagged the clipping from her hand. At a glance, he realized it was an article he knew well. He'd read it countless times, probably had it mostly memorized. The headline Game Warden Killed in the Line of Duty ran across the top. The article was a tidy account of his father's murder.

His father's unsolved murder.

The walls seemed to close in on him as he stared down at the familiar text.

"Why would you hide an article about my dad?" He was so shocked, so confused, he didn't even try to keep the accusation out of his tone.

She shook her head. "I'm not sure." She peeked inside the envelope again. Pulled out another sheet of paper. Her eyes widened and her hand flew to her mouth.

"What is it?" he asked.

"It's a photocopy," she explained. "It looks like an old Polaroid. You can see the white frame around it."

He reached for it.

"It's bad, Jude. I can't imagine why I have it."

Curiosity burned through him as he grabbed the second sheet of paper. He felt his eyes nearly pop when he realized what he was looking at.

"Someone poached a bald eagle," he growled. "And had the nerve to take a picture of it." His eyes lifted to her. "Bald eagles are protected under the Bald and Golden Eagle Protection Act. Intentionally poaching a bald eagle can result in an astronomical fine along with prison time." He waved the photo in the air. "Whoever this is, they can't get away with this." He lowered the photo, narrowed his gaze at her. "I'm a game warden, Ella. It's my job to go after people who do this kind of thing. Why would you have a photo like this, evidence of a felony, and not tell me?"

Bald eagles hadn't been on the endangered species list for two decades, but they were still federally protected. Poaching them broke all kinds of laws.

Frustration burned through him. The past few days, he'd allowed his not-quite-dead feelings for Ella stir back to life. But this, this photo, brought about new feelings of betrayal.

She tossed her hands in the air. "Do not ask me why I have it! You know I don't know."

"Are you protecting someone?" he demanded.

"No!" The word shot out of her mouth. She shook her head forcefully.

He raised an eyebrow at her, in question or disbelief, he wasn't sure. Probably both, which only caused her to protest more.

"Jude, you can't possibly think I'd cover up a crime like that."

"And yet," he said, his tone hardening as he pointed at the cookie jar, "covering it up, tucking it away, is exactly what you did." He huffed out a breath. "I can't believe you, Ella. Why would you do this?"

She bit her bottom lip and shook her head miserably.

He knew she didn't know why. Didn't remember why, anyway. But that didn't ease the feeling of betrayal—betrayal over her hiding someone's crime from him.

He dropped his gaze again, taking in every detail of the grisly picture this time. The majestic bird was being held up by his impressive wingspan. Its signature white head drooped to the side. It was obvious from his form that it was a man who was holding the bird. However, the photo was cut off mid-chin.

His heart pounded as he continued to study the photo. He searched for any type of distinguishing mark. A mole on the man's neck. A scar on an arm. There was nothing. From what little he could see of the man's frame, what the bird wasn't blocking, he thought he looked average size. Maybe even a bit on the small side.

It wasn't much.

But it might be something to go on.

Jude lowered the photo, preparing to study the newspaper clipping again. He paused, then lifted the photo up, studying it more intently than ever.

"What are you looking at?" Ella asked.

His heart clenched in his chest. This discovery might be so much bigger than he'd first anticipated. He sucked in a gulp of air because the realization of what he was looking at felt like it had knocked the breath from his lungs.

"This." He pointed out what he'd discovered in the photo.

"I was studying the perpetrator before. I wasn't paying attention to the location. Look at the area over his shoulder."

"There's a lake behind him." Ella met his gaze and all he saw there was confusion. That made two of them. Why did she have this? Where did she get it? Who was the man in the photo?

Because realization had hit him hard, nearly knocking him to his knees.

"Look here." Jude swallowed down the lump of dread building in his throat, tapped at the scene on the far shore. There wasn't much of it in the frame. "I know this spot."

With those words, he pivoted toward the door and rushed out of the kitchen. The location in the photo was one he knew well. One he would never forget.

He couldn't forget. Not when his father had died there.

He could hear Ella hustling behind him.

"If this photo was taken where I think it was taken," Jude said with a slight tremble in his voice, "then I think that, after all these years, we have the first clue as to who killed my dad."

Ella's heart ached as she noted the pain etched across Jude's face. He'd driven to the Pinecrest Landing, a small access for boats on the north end of Grace Lake, a tiny lake known for its trout.

And prime nesting grounds for bald eagles.

Also known for being the murder site of Landon Sheridan, Jude's father.

The landscape was similar enough to the photo to be identifiable, yet had changed over the years. Ella had to assume it stirred up old memories Jude would rather forget.

His gaze lifted to the treetops, scanning automatically. The game warden in him was still alert despite the pain she could see written in the tight lines of his face. A lone eagle circled above, its call piercing the quiet.

Ella wanted to go to him. Wanted to wrap her arms around him, take away some of his pain. Assure him that everything was going to be okay. But she didn't think he would appreciate her offer of comfort. She wasn't even sure he wanted her anywhere near him right now.

Her fingers curled into fists at her sides, nails digging into her palms as she fought the urge to reach for him.

The bright fall foliage rustled in the wind, a few colorful leaves fluttering free and spiraling down. The sky was azure, cloudless, and reflected upon the surface of the lake, making it look pristine.

It felt like far too beautiful of a day to be facing such an ugly past.

"This is it," Jude said.

His voice cracked slightly, grief slipping through despite his efforts to hold it back.

He held up the photocopy, comparing it to the view across the water.

Ella studied it along with him. Though the trees had grown taller with time, and the house in the photo had been added onto, turning it into an enormous lakeshore monstrosity, there was no doubt that the photo had been taken here.

"This is the place."

He turned to her, holding both the photocopy of the Polaroid and the newspaper clipping in his hands.

"It can't be coincidence that you hid these together. A newspaper clipping of my father's murder, along with a crime committed in this very spot. How did you piece this together?"

"I don't know that I did," Ella said.

But he didn't seem to hear her.

"Who is this? Who is in this photo?" He held it up, his tone, his expression, begging for answers. Not just from her, but maybe from God. She could only imagine how many prayers he had lifted up to the Father, begging for answers over the years.

When she could only shrug helplessly, he turned from her.

She watched him carefully, saw how his gaze swept the shoreline, like it always had when he was working—monitoring wildlife, keeping the peace. But now, the peace was gone from his face. He turned toward her again, his eyes filled with raw desperation.

His jaw tightened, a muscle feathering as he fought for control. His fists clenched around the papers.

She knew not knowing had weighed on not just him, but his entire family.

She wanted to answer him. She did. The entire drive to this spot she had pressed her memory, tried to dig deep.

Tried to come up with something. Anything.

Her effort had been in vain. Her memory still bore a gaping hole.

"Where did you get these? Especially the photo?" Jude demanded, his voice rough, cracking with emotion.

Ella felt the weight of guilt pressing down on her because she wondered that very same thing.

How could she do such a thing? Why? *Why* would she do such a thing? Even to her, it seemed cruel to hide such a blatant clue.

"You know I don't have an answer for that."

She took a step toward him, wanting to offer him comfort.

He took a step away.

She didn't blame him.

"I want answers as badly as you."

"I doubt that," he said with a shake of his head, his tone biting, distrust flashing in his eyes. "My family has wondered for years what led to my father's death." He pinched the bridge of his nose and closed his eyes.

His breathing was ragged, his shoulders bowed under the heavy burden of resurfaced grief.

She knew he was upset and trying to ground himself.

Of course, he was upset. How could he not be?

His father had been killed when Jude was nineteen.

All those years filled with unanswered questions.

Ella knew that not knowing had worn on the family, though they'd tried to move on.

Jude opened his eyes, narrowed them as he gazed at her.

"Are you sure you're not protecting someone?" he asked, his voice low and suspicious.

"What?" She stared back at him in surprise.

He echoed the question, his tone slow and deliberate this time. "Are you protecting someone?"

"Who would I possibly be protecting?" she demanded.

Hurt and surprise wove through her tone, though she realized that perhaps it was a legitimate question. She had to have had some reason for not sharing what she knew. Protecting someone sounded as logical as anything.

"I don't know," he said, his voice cold now, as he stared across the lake. "But I sure wish you could tell me."

She sighed and tugged a hand through her windblown hair.

Her mind was a blank slate.

When it came to the past few months, no matter how much she mentally prodded, there was just nothing there.

"Maybe this isn't how it looks," she said. "Maybe the article and the photo aren't related."

"Then why would you have them together?" he asked, his voice sharp.

She shrugged helplessly. "Looking at the photo in my kitchen, I had no idea the significance. I knew this was where your dad died," she said quietly. "But I don't think I would've pieced it together on my own. I don't think I ever would've realized that this was the spot in the photo. I've never been here before."

"*Someone* pieced it together." He turned from her and strode away.

She had to hurry to keep up.

"Where are you going?"

"We're taking this to Detective Chen. Maybe we should've met her first, but I just had to see, had to know for sure this was the same spot. There's no doubt," he said over the hood of his truck. "I can't prove that photo was taken the same day that my dad was killed, but I don't think it's a fluke that the newspaper article and the photo were found together. They have to be tied together."

Jude's posture was rigid with a new sense of urgency. Every movement had an edge, as if the adrenaline wouldn't let him stand still.

Once inside, he fired up the engine. Tires crunched on gravel as they pulled out of the access and onto the road.

"No one could ever pin down a motive for his murder," Jude said, more to himself than to her. "After months went by, we finally decided we had to accept that he was just in the wrong place at the wrong time. That his death was a random tragedy. But if he walked up on whoever was taking this photo, if he was just doing his job, he would've tried to take them in." He tapped the envelope resting on the console, once again holding the evidence inside. "This person was clearly armed since they shot the eagle. It makes sense now. It's wrong," he rasped out. "So very wrong. But after all these years it finally makes sense."

Jude was so distraught over the discovery, and Ella so distraught over Jude, that neither of them noticed the black, oversized sedan that had gained on them when they crested the hill.

Ella spotted the movement out of the side-view mirror at nearly the same time Jude glanced into the rearview mirror.

"Jude?" she said, her tone a sharp warning.

"Yeah, I see them," he murmured darkly as the vehicle closed the distance between them.

The sedan clipped Jude's bumper on the passenger side as they rounded a curve in the road, causing the truck to spin toward the other lane.

Ella let out a shriek of surprise as Jude fought to keep the truck from fishtailing.

It was a losing battle.

The tires squealed, the truck jostled and bumped as it skidded, going sideways, cutting across the oncoming lane directly in front of a car that was heading their way.

"Hold on!" Jude shouted.

Please, God! she silently cried. The simple plea encompassed a complex prayer that she trusted God would understand.

Her parents' faces flashed through her mind, then Jude's, then the terrified strangers in the silver car barreling toward them.

Please keep us from colliding with the oncoming car.

Please keep us safe.

Please keep the car's passengers safe.

Please let us get out of this alive!

She didn't want anyone else to be harmed because of her.

Ella pushed back in her seat, trying to brace for impact as the truck careened over the edge.

The silver car, horn blaring, spliced between Jude's truck and the black sedan that had rammed them.

Then they were airborne.

ELEVEN

Jude gritted his teeth as the truck slammed into the ground, then bounced off a tree as it hit the embankment. The airbag deployed, crashing into him, knocking the breath from his body. He heard Ella sputter something under her breath, probably a prayer, as her airbag also smacked into her.

His bones felt as if they rattled as the truck flipped, rolled. His mind silently cried out to his Creator to watch over them, keep them safe even as the vehicle continued to jostle them. The fear in his chest grew, each violent lurch of the truck making him wonder if this would be the last one. Would they survive the next roll?

With a final thud, the truck bounced, then stilled in a heap of crunched metal and shattered glass. But silence, such unnerving silence, followed, pressing in like a heavy weight. The world outside felt distant, as if the air itself had frozen.

The engine had cut off when the airbag deployed. For a moment, the only sound Jude could hear was the blood sloshing through his ears as his heart pounded frantically.

He took an instant mental inventory of himself. Though his bones felt jarred and his thoughts discombobulated from the flipping and the rolling, he didn't think he'd suffered anything more damaging than some bruising. His chest ached from where his seat belt had held him in place, and he was grateful for it.

But his senses screamed at him that something was wrong. He couldn't shake the feeling that they were not alone anymore.

His thoughts quickly looped around to his passenger.

Despite the airbag, he managed to twist his head to the side. He tried to reach out to Ella but the airbag was in the way. They had landed on a hillside, propped against a tree. The truck was sitting at an angle that would send Jude crashing down onto Ella, crushing her, if it wasn't for the seat belt and airbag holding him tight.

She was facing him, her eyes closed, her face scrunched. In pain? In anticipation of another flip?

"Ella!" he cried, silently praying she was okay.

Her eyes fluttered. She blinked hard, then her gaze locked on to his.

"Are you hurt?" he demanded.

"I'm okay," she said, her voice shaky. She paused, then said, "Just need to catch my breath."

The vulnerability in her voice sent a jolt of dread through him. He'd been so angry with her at the lake, and though he was still angry, he was grateful that she was okay and that their fight wasn't the last conversation they would ever have.

"How's your head?" he asked. He couldn't believe she'd just lived through another rollover.

"The airbag held me in place." She paused a moment, as if assessing. "I'm fine. Sore, but fine."

He nodded, groping around for his seat-belt buckle. "We need to get out of here. Can you get your buckle undone?"

Every second felt like an eternity. His mind screamed at him that they had no time to waste.

Ella seemed to pick up on the tension in his tone and began

to feel around for her buckle as well. He couldn't help envisioning the man creeping down the hill, gun drawn, ready to murder him and Ella in cold blood as they were trapped helplessly in his truck. He forced away the thought. They couldn't afford to be paralyzed by fear. But it lingered, gnawing at the back of his mind.

That wasn't going to happen. He worked his feet around, finding traction.

"You think he'll come after us," Ella said, her tone taking on an edge of panic. It wasn't a question, and he didn't respond, but that's exactly what he thought. Sitting here, trapped, he couldn't help but feel that danger was closing in.

"Can we get out through your door?" he asked. He braced himself, pressing his feet hard against the floorboard as he disengaged his seat belt, to ensure he wouldn't topple into her. It would be easier to go out her door, rather than fight gravity to climb out of his.

She worked her head around. "No. There's a tree. The door is pinned against it. I think it's what stopped us from rolling again."

A sense of urgency twisted in his gut. Would they make it out before something worse happened?

He heard the click of Ella's seat belt. Was aware that she was disentangling herself from it, working to squirm it around the airbag that was slowly deflating.

He was also hyperaware of how much time had passed since they'd rolled. How much time did they have before their pursuer was upon them?

"We'll get out my side. The incline is enough to make it a bit tough, but I don't think we're in danger of rolling again. Once we're out, we'll run into the trees." Away from the road. Away from potential danger. His cell phone was in his jacket pocket. He'd use it once they were hidden because he sure didn't have time for it now.

Sweat streamed down his brow. He swiped at it, only to see it wasn't sweat. The back of his hand was smeared with a thick layer of blood. He realized he must've been cut by shattered window glass. Once he'd touched the wound, it began to throb, adrenaline having masked it before. Regardless, he needed to get moving. Needed to get them out of there.

Before it was too late.

He shoved his door open and gravity invited it to slam shut again. He managed to stop it with one hand, but his heart stuttered in his chest. From the new angle, the door propped half-open, he spotted movement in the side-view mirror attached to the door.

Motorcycle boots appeared. Jean-clad legs took cautious steps down the hillside. Jude dug around frantically, trying to free his pistol from his holster. The airbag was a floppy mess he had to maneuver around.

The boots moved closer. Slowly. Carefully.

His pulse raced. How close were they? Was he already too late to take the shot?

That portion of the hill was steep, probably difficult to traverse.

The pursuer probably correctly assumed he was armed. Was that why their approach was so cautious?

"Stay here until I tell you to get out," Jude ordered.

After bracing his right foot next to the gearshift, he shoved hard, propelling himself out of the seat. He emerged through the open door, reached into his jacket and scrabbled for his gun, preparing to take aim. Hoping to take the person by surprise.

He froze, half-in, half-out of the door, propped against the doorframe. His hand tucked under his jacket when he realized who was navigating the hill.

Next to the guy in motorcycle boots—a young guy, Jude realized, now that he could see his face—was a petite blonde, her ponytail bouncing with every step. The pair, a teenage couple by the look of it, startled when Jude appeared. Their eyes went wide, and their expressions showed evident relief that they weren't approaching a vehicle containing mangled bodies.

The sudden shift from dread to confusion left him reeling. Who were these kids, and what had they seen?

The girl was wearing flip-flops and the guy was guiding her down by gently holding her arm. No wonder they were going so slow.

"Hi! Hey, are you okay?" the girl asked.

He heard Ella gasp. From her position in the truck, she hadn't been aware that anyone was approaching.

"Jude?" Ella's tone was full of questions.

Jude nearly collapsed in relief, but the girl prattled on, not allowing him to speak. She put some hustle in her step now that she'd spotted him and said, "My name is Hillary. This is Damian. We're here to help you. Are you hurt? You shouldn't move. Just sit still. Help is on the way. Oh, my. You are hurt. You're bleeding." She whipped off the white silk scarf she wore around her neck. "You need to put some pressure on that cut," she said, moving in so quickly that she had the scarf pressed against his wound before he could protest.

Jude blinked at her in stunned silence for just one moment. Somebody appeared to have passed their first-aid training with flying colors.

"Uh, thanks," he said, gently pushing her hand away. "But we really need to get out of here." He placed one foot on the ground, pulled the other foot free from the vehicle. He stumbled, caught himself on the door. He felt woozy and wasn't sure if it was from the tumble down the hill, the head wound, or the realization that they weren't going to be shot at.

At least, not by this pair.

"Hey, man, maybe you should sit," Damian said as he took Jude's elbow.

Jude was tempted to shake the guy off, but knew he was only trying to help.

"I'm okay," Jude said. "I need to get my friend out."

"There's someone else in there?" Hillary asked. Without waiting for an answer, she darted past him, poking her head into the truck.

His thoughts raced. Who were these people, really? Were they truly there to help, or was this just another twist in their already tangled nightmare?

Ella, apparently having decided his command to stay put was null and void with the appearance of the teens, appeared in the doorframe, nearly smacking heads with Hillary.

"Oh, what a relief!" Hillary cried. "You're okay, too. We called for help. An ambulance is on the way."

Damian finally released Jude's arm and the two of them moved toward the truck. Together they managed to help Ella to the ground. Jude's grip held on after Damian let go. Ella trembled as she stood beside him.

"The other vehicle," she began as her gaze scanned the road above. "Where did they go?"

"Those jerks that ran you off the road?" Damian asked.

"They took off," Hillary said, her scowl matching the disgust in her tone.

"Did you get a good look at the vehicle?" Jude asked. "Notice any identifying details? Make? Model?"

"Uh..." Damian glanced at Hillary, who shrugged. "No, I guess not. It was a big black car. I'd guess it was older but couldn't give you a year. Not even sure what make it was. That's all I noticed."

"We just saw it coming at you and it pretty much freaked us out," Hillary said. "I wasn't really paying attention to the details."

"Nothing?" Jude persisted.

"Sorry," Hillary replied. "It was all I could do to drive between the two of you and not go off the road myself."

"You did great," Damian murmured.

She flashed him a smile. "Thanks."

"You're sure they didn't stop?" Ella asked. "They didn't turn back around?"

Jude knew she was worried about the safety of these kids. She didn't want them to be caught in the crosshairs of this mess.

"Positive," Hillary said. "They zipped on by. Didn't come back while I was calling for help. They seemed pretty intent on getting out of here." She gave them a sympathetic smile. "Some people are just jerks. I was rear-ended once. The guy took off. The cops found him later and he didn't have insurance. That's why he fled. It turned into a big disaster."

Jude gave her a tight smile. If lack of insurance was the only issue here, he'd be a happy guy.

The faint shriek of sirens grabbed his attention.

"See?" Hillary said brightly. "Help is on the way."

"Thank you," Ella said.

"Hopefully they'll stitch you right up," Hillary said to Jude.

Ella whirled on him, her gaze zooming into the gash on his head. She grabbed his chin, tilting his face so she could get a good look. "You're hurt!"

Yeah.

Apparently, she'd missed that while concentrating on maneuvering out of the vehicle.

"I told him to press this to the wound," Hillary said as she held up her soiled scarf by the clean end.

Ella tugged it from the girl's grip. "Thank you," she said to Hillary. To Jude, she ordered, "Do what the girl said."

With a sigh, he took the scarf and pressed it to the cut, trying not to wince at the pain the pressure caused.

"Let's get up this hill," he decided. "No sense just standing here."

"Just a minute," Ella said. She scrambled backward, peering into the truck again. "I need to get something."

The envelope.

With the evidence.

He decided taking a tumble in his truck had scrambled his brain more than he'd realized.

That should've been his first thought. They needed to get the information to Detective Chen immediately. Though he still wasn't sure he trusted the woman's skills, she was their best hope at getting some answers.

They had to start somewhere.

Ella swayed when her feet hit the ground again and he knew he wasn't the only one feeling the effects of the crash.

Together the four of them climbed the hill. Damian's attention was focused on Hillary. Keeping her feet in her flip-flops was even more of a challenge on the way up than it had been on the way down.

Jude was glad the pair were distracted. Though they'd assured him the vehicle that pushed them off the road was long gone, he was hypervigilant as they climbed, prepared for the thugs to strike at any moment. His hand cradled his weapon, though he didn't withdraw it.

Ella trudged up the hill beside him, wearing a grim look.

He was aware of traffic on the road ahead as cars slowed, likely to get around Hillary's vehicle, which he could see parked on the slim shoulder, before they continued on.

He was aware that above them, a vehicle had stopped.

Could be gawkers.

Could be another Good Samaritan, like Hillary.

As the sirens neared, the wailing turning into shrieks, he wasn't nearly as concerned that their attackers would risk coming back.

They crested the hill and he nearly collapsed in relief at the sight of emergency vehicles pulling to a stop in front of them.

Ella's arm ached from where it had slammed into the passenger door, jarred by the impact of hitting the tree. She would have a dandy of a bruise, but nothing appeared to be broken. Her chest ached something fierce as the lifesaving seat belt had held her in place yet again.

Apparently, road rage was their attacker's MO.

Jude had refused stitches, instead opting for a butterfly bandage offered up by the EMT in the ambulance that had arrived on-site. The cut hadn't been as bad as Ella had feared, despite how badly it had bled.

Jude's vehicle was totaled, and when they'd left the scene, a tow truck had set to work towing it up the hill. An officer had driven them back to Jude's ranch. Jude had barely spoken to her, and she hadn't pushed it, assuming he needed time to process what they'd discovered at the landing.

They'd given their statements at the scene, as had Hillary and Damian, and now they were waiting for Detective Chen, who had been held up in town at the site of the shooting.

She felt battered both physically and emotionally. She was

sure Jude must be regretting letting her back into his life. What a fiasco the last few days had been.

Perhaps, Ella thought, she should drain her savings and leave town. She could come back from financial ruin. She could not come back from being dead. Whoever was after her was proving to be relentless.

Knowing they were willing to hurt—even kill—Jude to get to her was unacceptable. When she'd accepted his offer to help, she hadn't expected to put his life in danger. Not just once, but multiple times.

As Lexie paced Jude's living room, she made it clear that she had the exact same thought.

"I was worried about you breaking my brother's heart again," she grumbled at Ella. "I didn't realize I should be worried about you getting him killed. You almost got his house burned down, he was shot at and now, his truck is destroyed."

"I have insurance," Jude said. "No one got killed. That's what really matters."

"This time!" Lexie retorted. "Clearly, these men aren't going to stop until Ella's dead…or they're caught. I don't want you to be collateral damage."

"Lexie," Jude growled.

"No," Ella said, "she's right. When you offered to let me stay here, I had no idea these men would be so aggressive. Maybe I should head out of town until they're caught."

Lexie perked up at the suggestion. "Where will you go?"

Jude heaved out a heavy sigh. "She's not going anywhere."

The front door creaked open before banging closed again. Everyone's attention swiveled to Blake, who now stood in the entryway. Ella had been so wrapped up in her thoughts, and the conversation, that she hadn't heard him drive up. He'd spent enough time at Jude's that he obviously felt comfortable letting himself in.

He strode into the room like he owned the place. "What's going on here? I leave you alone, and the two of you can't stay out of trouble for even a few hours?" he said, fuming. "First, you get shot at. Then, as if that weren't enough, you get yourself into a wreck?"

Actually, Ella thought, they didn't get themselves into a wreck. Their pursuers did that. She didn't think it would ease Blake's temper any to argue with him.

"Blake," Jude said, his tone soothing, "I thought you were off duty. What are you doing here? Shouldn't you be catching up on sleep?"

"I was," he grumbled. "But I got hungry. Got up to get myself a sandwich. Had the police scanner on in the kitchen. I didn't even have time to pull the bread out before I realized the two of you were in all sorts of trouble again."

"It's been a rough day," Jude agreed.

"You think?" Blake scoffed. He dropped down on the sofa next to Lexie. "You might as well catch me up."

Jude filled Blake and Lexie in on their run-in with Madison, the shooting and the accident.

He hadn't uttered a word about the photo or the newspaper clipping that had been in Ella's possession. She thought he probably didn't want to upset Lexie any more than she already was, but didn't doubt that he'd fill Blake in the minute he got him alone.

"Chief Zimmerman's daughter?" Blake asked, incredulous. He crossed his arms over his chest and leaned back into the cushions. "I've never heard of her being in any kind of trouble." His brow furrowed as he dug into his memory. "She just finished nursing school. She's an LPN. She went into that field because of her mom. If I remember correctly, she just started working at one of the nursing homes in town. She rotates between doing that and caring for her mom." He shook his head. "I don't remember which nursing home, though."

"It probably doesn't matter," Jude said. "A nursing home is hardly a hotbed for criminal activity."

Lexie tapped her fingers against her knee as she cut a suspicious look Ella's way. Ella mentally steeled herself for whatever Lexie was about to say.

"What if," she began, "we're looking at this all wrong?"

"How so?" Jude asked his sister.

Yes, Ella thought, *how so?*

"What if Ella went to Madison?" She held up a hand. "Hear me out. Maybe Ella got into some trouble and went to Madison for advice."

Ella shook her head. That didn't sound right. It didn't *feel* right. But what did she know?

"Maybe you accidentally purchased stolen antiques," Lexie suggested. "Or maybe someone shoplifted, and it was someone you knew so you didn't want them to get in too much trouble."

"I don't think someone would try to kill Ella over a shoplifting incident," Jude said.

"I was just throwing ideas out there." With a glance at her watch, Lexie got to her feet. "I hate working such odd shifts. I have to go or I'm going to be late." She moved toward the front door but stopped just short of it. She turned to face Ella and Jude. Swinging a finger between the two of them, she said, "For once, would you two try to stay out of trouble?"

"I'm not going anywhere," Blake said. "I'll look after them."

Ella noticed that it seemed as if it was all Jude could do to not roll his eyes at his friend. She knew Jude was completely competent, with or without Blake here. And while they'd faced numerous attacks that were out of their control, Jude had managed to keep them safe every time. Still, it definitely couldn't hurt to have Blake stick around.

Lexie gave a little wave, and then she was gone.

As Ella had suspected, Jude had been waiting for her to go.

"There's a whole lot more to the story," he said to Blake. "I just didn't want to talk about it in front of Lexie because it would upset her. She'd have questions that I just don't have answers to."

His gaze cut into Ella as he spoke.

She wanted to wither away. She understood he was upset with her for keeping such monumental information to herself. She could understand why he was upset. What she could not do was explain herself.

So while he filled in Blake, starting with the cookie jar and ending with the rollover, she listened in silence. All the while, she mentally prodded at her memory. It was to no avail, and all she got for her efforts was an overwhelming sense of frustration.

Please, God, restore my memory. I want to be able to give Jude the answers he needs.

"Let me see the picture," Blake said.

Jude slid it from the envelope and handed it, along with the clipping, to his friend.

Blake let out a low whistle as he studied the copy of the Polaroid. "Wow. It takes a special kind of arrogance to shoot a bald eagle and then have the nerve to take a picture."

"I know," Jude said quietly. "And someone who thought that highly of themselves, well, I could see them thinking their life is worth more than Dad's was. That kind of person could be capable of killing a man to save his own hide."

Blake turned to Ella, his expression hard. "You mean to

tell me you had possession of evidence that could potentially solve Jude's father's murder and you kept it to yourself?"

"I don't know," Ella began, guilt eating at her once again. "I guess it looks that way. But—"

Jude cut her off as he nodded toward the picture window, which he was facing. "Looks like Detective Chen just pulled up."

"Can't wait to hear what she thinks about this," Blake said. "Maybe it'll give her the clue she needs to finally solve your dad's murder."

"That's what I'm hoping, too," Jude said as he hoisted himself to his feet. He winced as he made his way to the door, and Ella realized he was just as banged up from the accident as she was. He was just better at hiding it. Most of the time.

He greeted Detective Chen at the door, then motioned toward the chair he'd just vacated. She took it while he settled on the sofa next to Blake.

The detective's gaze bore into her. "It appears we have an awful lot of catching up to do."

"Yes," Ella said. "I think you're right. Quite a bit has happened since we last spoke."

The detective reiterated what she already knew about the shooting and the accident.

"What I don't understand," Detective Chen said, "is what you were doing out on Kestrel Road."

"You need to take a look at these," Blake said. He handed the newspaper and photocopy to the detective. "There's a whole lot more to this story."

Detective Chen's gaze scanned over the article, then the photo. Her expression remained frustratingly impassive. Finally, she lifted her gaze to Ella. "Where did you find these?"

"In my cookie jar," Ella said a bit sheepishly. "I realize I need to invest in a safe," she added. "But the important thing here is that if you look closely at the photo, it's at the site where Jude's father was killed."

"Ella should have handed this over to you immediately," Blake said. "Now, she can't remember where they came from."

"Detective," Jude said slowly, "you don't seem particularly surprised by the photo." He leaned forward, studying the woman's face.

She placed the papers on the coffee table. "I'm not. I've seen them before."

Ella heard Jude's sharp intake of breath, but the detective continued before he could interrupt her.

"Ella, I've been keeping something from you," Chen said.

Ella's heart skipped a beat, and she shared a quick, confused glance with Jude.

The detective rose to her feet and began to pace the room. "I've been keeping something from all of you. Not to be deceptive," she said, keeping her voice firm, "but because I thought it was in Ella's best interest. I know that it's best to let amnesia patients regain their memories on their own. I didn't want to disclose something that Ella would find shocking. But now—" she let her gaze scan over the small group, "—I feel I can't keep the truth from you any longer. Not when lives are on the line."

"What is it?" Ella asked, her heart in her throat.

Detective Chen pulled in a breath, straightened her shoulders, then said, "Ella, you've been working as a confidential informant."

"Wh-what?" Ella stammered, Chen's words having hit her with the force of a tidal wave she hadn't seen coming.

"It's true, Ella," Detective Chen said. "You've been working as a confidential informant...*for me*."

TWELVE

Jude bolted upright from the edge of the couch, his heart pounding. Ella? His sweet, gentle, antique-loving Ella could not be a confidential informant. He had to have heard wrong, or misunderstood. "I'm sorry. What did you just say?"

Detective Chen's voice was calm. Too calm. "You heard me correctly."

The air seemed to drain from the room. Suddenly, Jude felt as if he couldn't breathe. Outside, sleet tapped steadily against the windows, a cold, rhythmic percussion that echoed the sudden frost creeping through his veins. The fire crackled in the hearth nearby, logs popping as flames danced in a blaze of warmth that felt cruelly at odds with the conversation unraveling in the room.

"I don't understand," he said, his voice tight.

He glanced at Ella, but of course, with her memory absent, she looked as confused as he felt.

"I don't remember that," she whispered.

Jude turned to Chen. "Did you figure it out then? Do you know who killed my dad? Who is it?" He took a step toward the door, every nerve screaming to find this person and bring them to justice.

"Sit down," Blake said firmly from across the room.

"You're not leaving this house. Not until you're thinking clearly."

Jude ignored him and turned to Chen. "Someone murdered my dad. And you've known something this big and didn't say a word?"

"Let her start from the beginning," Blake said calmly.

Jude knew he was right, but calm was the last thing he was feeling right now. His body tensed, heart hammering in his chest. The storm outside picked up, wind howling faintly beyond the walls. He dropped his hand from the doorknob and leaned against the doorframe, fists clenched.

Jaclyn continued. "This past summer, Ella came to me. She found something strange in her shop—a handcrafted jewelry box, walnut with bronze accents. No price tag. It wasn't on her inventory list. She said it wasn't something she remembered ever seeing before."

He glanced at Ella, watching her struggle, likely in vain, to remember. She was staring off, as if into the past, her brow furrowed, her expression intense.

"Inside the box were two things," she continued. "First, a Polaroid photo. A man holding a dead bald eagle. His face was mostly cropped and much of his body obscured behind the wings. Ella didn't recognize the background, but I did. Immediately. It was the Pinecrest Landing. The very spot your father was killed."

Jude felt the floor tilt.

"The second item was a newspaper clipping," Jaclyn said. "The front page from the day after your father died. A small-town game warden gunned down, no suspects. Just those two things in that box. No note. No fingerprints. But deliberate. Precise clues, but not nearly enough to go on."

Jude turned to Ella, his tone accusing. "Why didn't you tell me?"

"She wanted to," Jaclyn answered, because she—and everyone in the room—knew Ella couldn't. "She came to me first because she thought maybe it was a hoax, a cruel joke someone planted in her store. She felt it wasn't right to bring it to your attention until she knew whether or not it held value. As soon as I looked everything over, I realized the significance." Chen held her head high, unapologetic. "I asked her to keep it from you."

"Why?" Jude demanded.

"Why do you think?" Detective Chen asked.

He didn't have to answer out loud. He would have gone out on his own, desperate for answers, and would have tried to find those answers himself. Of course, she would want to be the one to dig into this decade-old crime. It had been her case to solve all those years ago. She was probably worried he'd barge in, desperate to solve his father's murder and muck it all up.

"You were rattled, and rightfully so," Chen told Ella. "You hadn't told Jude. You were afraid of hurting him or getting his hopes up if it turned out to be nothing. But you were also convinced that the jewelry box was planted intentionally. That it wasn't part of your inventory by accident. And I had every reason to believe you were right. You wanted to tell Jude, but I didn't think it was a good idea. I begged you to give me some time to figure this out, but keeping this secret from him, it was rough on you. I took the box and started doing some research. The craftsmanship was unique, modern—not antique. I tracked the artisan stamp on the underside to Ellington Designs in Bozeman. After some back-and-forth, they confirmed the box had been a commissioned piece—handcrafted for Vivian Lorraine Zimmerman. VLZ. Her initials, which are a bit unique, were lightly engraved on the bottom."

Jude straightened. "Madison's mom."

"Exactly," Chen said. "It was purchased by Chief Zimmerman, according to the design records, which are kept on file for each special order. And suddenly, I had two connections. First, a photo taken at a murder scene. Second, a custom box that originated from the chief's household."

Jude moved to the couch and sat down abruptly, his knees threatening to buckle. He was infinitely glad that Lexie had left for work. This would be hard enough to explain to her later, but it would be better coming from him.

He propped his elbows on his knees as he focused on breathing and listening to the detective.

"But the real twist," she added, "came from the photo. When I enlarged it, I noticed a faint emblem on the man's shirt."

"I studied that photo," Jude said. "I didn't notice that." Had he missed it? He was no detective, but he did have a criminal-justice background. It irked him that he'd missed something. He reached for the photo.

"I have the original," Chen said. "I didn't realize Ella made a copy."

Ella gave a tiny shrug.

Jude studied the scene again. There, just behind the eagle wing, was a fuzzy gray area. It could be an emblem, but with the picture quality, it was hard to tell.

"The original is a bit clearer, though not by much. I had a friend of mine, a tech at another department, enlarge the photo and enhance the clarity," she explained. "From there, I could tell it was a race logo. I recognized it from a Police Unity Fund Marathon held the summer your dad died. One of our officers had been diagnosed with cancer, and the department put together a fundraiser to help with medical expenses that year."

"Sounds like a pretty solid clue," Blake interjected.

"I started combing through archived race photos," Chen continued, "department rosters and event registration logs. That emblem, barely visible, narrowed the field of suspects. Not conclusively, but enough to make me dig deeper into the chief's possible involvement. He'd been an officer for several years, but he wasn't the chief at that time."

Jude blew out a breath. He stared at the fire, watching the flames snap and leap. The warmth should have brought comfort, but it only made the cold tension in his chest more unbearable.

"Still," she said, "I didn't have proof. Only suspicions. That's when I asked Ella to get close to Madison. To see if anything would shake loose."

"She agreed," Jude said.

"Yes, but she knew you were already suspicious. After a day of deliberating, she decided it would be best to break off your engagement while we worked everything out. She thought that would be better than facing you every day, lying to you when you would press her about what was bothering her. It would also free up some of her time to spend with Madison."

Jude remembered those days before the breakup. Ella had been on edge. She'd been withdrawn and had even canceled a dinner date. So, yeah, he'd realized something wasn't right.

His gaze met Ella's across the room. She looked apologetic and…sad.

At least now, he had his answer—they both did. Well, one answer, anyway. They knew why Ella had broken off the engagement, but honestly, he couldn't think about that now. For months, he'd wanted an answer.

But there was another answer he'd been waiting even longer for.

The world seemed to swim in front of Jude's eyes. All these years he'd been so angry with Detective Chen for not solving his dad's murder. When really, was there someone else in the department who was even more to blame?

"Do you think the chief killed my father?" he rasped out.

Detective Chen's expression was hard, but her eyes glistened faintly. She blinked fast. "I think I need more evidence before I can make that call. I need something more than my hunch to go on if charges are going to stick. You know that."

Ella wrapped her arms around herself as if trying to physically brace against the emotions created by this conversation. "And I was part of that?" she asked softly, her voice breaking. "I was using Madison, trying to get close to her?" She hesitated. "I don't understand why. Do you think she knows something?"

Jaclyn nodded. "I'm hoping so. You narrowed down the time frame when the jewelry box likely appeared, and I was able to get surveillance footage from the bakery across the street. During that window, a woman entered your store carrying a large bag. She wasn't inside long, just a minute or two, then she hurried back out."

She paused. "The footage is black-and-white and not great quality, and the woman was wearing a hat and sunglasses, but I believe it was Madison."

"You think she planted the jewelry box," Jude said.

"I suspect it. But only because I'd already connected the jewelry box to her mother before seeing the footage. The video alone wouldn't be enough to make that call—the woman's face is mostly obscured, but her build is similar to Madison's. She would have access to the jewelry box and the time frame fit."

She continued, "Ella was at an estate sale at the time. When she asked Marjorie about customers that day, Marjorie mentioned a woman who came in while she was helping someone else and left before she could speak with her. I think Madison used that brief window to leave the jewelry box on a shelf near the front. She was probably hoping Ella would notice it right away…and she did."

"Have you called in the state police yet?" Blake asked, his voice tight with suspicion.

"I have not," Jaclyn admitted. "Before you ask why, think about it."

Blake's lips twisted into a frown. "If you accuse the chief, and he's innocent, you'll never live it down."

"More than that," Jaclyn said, her voice low and serious, "I'd be tarnishing a man's reputation. I need to be sure. Or as close to sure as I can be. I've been compiling information and I have every intention of handing it over, as soon as I have something substantive. Right now, everything I have is circumstantial."

Jude felt his gut tighten with frustration, but Jaclyn continued, her gaze unwavering.

"You don't understand the weight of this, Jude. If I reach out to the state police and let them investigate the chief, it could start a chain reaction. Even if I try to keep it quiet, these things always have a way of coming out. The moment anyone in the state department gets wind of it, it could be all over town in a matter of days. The chief's reputation is everything here, and we can't risk it being destroyed on a hunch."

Blake crossed his arms, his voice taking on a more thoughtful tone. "What's the real risk, Jaclyn? The man could be guilty, and he's walking free. Don't you think that's more important than his reputation?"

Jaclyn shook her head slowly, her expression suddenly filled with uncertainty. "You're right, Blake. But this isn't just about a man's guilt or innocence. It's about a career built over decades. The chief's not just any officer. He's a pillar of this community. People trust him, look up to him. If this investigation becomes public, even if we find out he's innocent, it'll be impossible to restore his standing. The damage will be done. People will question everything he's ever done, every decision he's ever made." She shook her head, hesitating, clearly debating. "But if you want the honest truth, I'm afraid if he catches whispers about what I'm doing, he'll bury any remnants of evidence, any chance I have of solving this case so deep, that we'll never get justice."

Jude leaned forward, his eyes narrowing as he processed her words. "So what's the alternative? We just wait until there's enough evidence to charge him, even if he's been walking around with blood on his hands this whole time?"

Jaclyn met his gaze, her voice low but firm. "We play this carefully. We continue to gather the evidence, make sure it's airtight. And then, if it points to him, we act. The chief isn't some random suspect. He has decades of law-enforcement background."

"You think he outsmarted you once," Jude said, hoping the words didn't sound accusatory, "and you're afraid he'll do it again."

"I don't want to take any risks," Chen said. "I need ironclad proof."

"Sounds to me like you've spent months trying to get proof and have come up with nothing," Jude said bitterly. "So what do we do?"

Jaclyn met his gaze, her voice steady but firm. "We keep working the case. We find the evidence we need to make sure we can put him behind bars. If he's the guilty one."

"You have doubts?" Jude asked.

"I believe in following the law. Innocent until proven

guilty." She pulled in a breath. "And that means that right now, I really have my work cut out for me."

Ella sat motionless, absorbing every word Detective Chen said, her eyes flicking between the detective and Jude. She tracked every shift in Jude's expression. She saw confusion. Disbelief. Pain. The way his brow furrowed and his jaw clenched told her more than words ever could. None of what Chen said sparked recognition in her mind, yet she didn't doubt a word of it.

Still, it was odd to hear about her own life, as if she was an outsider. As if she had taken no part in it, when clearly she had.

A log popped in the fireplace, the sound grating against her already frayed nerves. She folded her hands in her lap, knuckles white.

Outside, sleet tapped sharply against the windowpane, a restless, needling sound that echoed the turmoil inside her. It reminded her of the way her thoughts battered against the blank walls of her mind, relentless and unanswered. She glanced at Jude again, at the shadow in his eyes and the tension in his jaw, and the ache returned. It was a hollow ache that came not from memory, but from absence.

She didn't remember the moment she'd walked away from him, but she felt the weight of it now. It clung to her like the cold, gray sky pressing in on the house.

"Was I helpful at all?" she asked, her voice barely above a whisper. What she really wanted to know, what she didn't dare ask, was if she had shattered Jude's heart for nothing.

Chen's voice gentled. "You were getting there. These things take time. It's not like you could bombard Madison with questions the first time you went to lunch. Or even the second. But you were making real progress."

Ella's breath hitched. "Progress how?"

"At first, Madison refused to meet with you. But then, you reached out again. You told her you were struggling with your dad's illness. You said you thought she might understand, given what her mother was going through. That's when she agreed to lunch. You started building trust. You tried forming a connection."

Ella's stomach churned. "Fake friends?" The question escaped sharper than she meant it to. She understood the reasoning behind it. But still, the idea of using someone, even someone potentially complicit in something terrible, sat heavily on her chest.

Chen didn't answer immediately. Then, gently, she said, "I think the friendship you formed became real. You talked about your dad. She opened up about her mom. And eventually, you began to ask more pointed questions—subtle ones—about her relationship with her stepfather. The chief. You said they didn't seem close. You thought Madison might actually resent him."

Chen's words brushed the edge of a memory just out of reach.

"But I didn't get a confession," she said quietly.

Jaclyn hesitated. Her gaze shifted to Jude before returning to Ella. "I'm not so sure about that."

Jude sat forward, and Ella could almost feel the tension emanating from him. He glanced at Ella, then back at Chen. "What do you mean?"

Chen exhaled. "I was out of town the day of Ella's…accident. But she called me that afternoon." Her eyes softened as she looked at Ella. "You said Madison was finally opening up. You told me you didn't want to say anything more over the phone. I was already heading back to Haven Creek to meet you when I got the call about the crash."

Ella's heart pounded. "You think I got a confession?"

"Either that, or you were close. Someone else obviously figured that out, because they went after you. It was no coincidence that someone ran you off the road that very day."

And someone had been after her every day since. Yes, it only made sense that she had uncovered something, or had come awfully close to it. There was no doubt in Ella's mind that Madison was somehow the center of it all.

"Do you know what I was doing on Sagebrush Bend that night?" Ella asked.

Chen nodded solemnly. "I believe you were going to see Jude. You told me you couldn't keep this from him any longer. You said you owed him the truth. I asked you to hold off, to give me a chance to confirm things after we spoke in person, but you said you couldn't. That he deserved to know everything."

Ella turned toward Jude. He was staring back at her, his expression unreadable, as if he was trying to piece together what she might have said, what she might have meant to tell him. She longed to reach for him, to bridge the gaping emotional space between them.

"None of this is familiar?" Jude asked, his tone level, almost flat. She knew he was trying not to press her, though he desperately wanted answers.

"I'm trying," she said miserably, the words breaking on a breath. "Trying to remember is all I've been doing for days."

"What it comes down to," Jude said, "is that Madison is the key to all of this."

"Yes," Chen agreed.

"Then I need to talk to her," Ella said. "If she confessed to me once, I'll have to make her do it again."

"What are you going to do?" Blake asked. "Just call her up and demand answers? We need to think this through. We need to come up with a plan, a way to convince her it's safe for her to tell you everything."

Jude raked a hand through his hair. "Okay. So how do we—"

Ella's phone rang, cutting him off. Her first thought was to ignore it, but her heart stuttered when she saw the name on the display. She held up her hand, stopping the conversation in the room.

"Hello, Madison?" she said.

"Ella," Madison said, her voice shaking. "I heard you were in another accident just this afternoon. Are you okay?"

"Yes, thank you for checking on me," Ella replied, her mind whirling as she tried to decide what to say next. How could she get a confession out of this friendship that she didn't remember?

"We need to talk," Madison said.

"I think so, too." Mixed emotions slammed into her. Surprise that Madison was reaching out to her, but maybe she'd had enough of the danger, too. Because clearly, she'd been on the defensive before the shooting in town. Hope that they would finally have the answers they'd been searching for. Determination that she would not let this opportunity pass her by.

"Can you meet me? Alone? I know you don't remember. But we're friends and I'm worried about you. I'm just not ready to face Jude yet," Madison admitted, her voice quiet and wobbly.

Ella held the phone away from her ear. Jude and Chen moved closer. Jude shook his head vehemently, while the detective gave her a firm nod.

"Yes, of course," Ella said. "Where? When?"

"Now? At the Pinecrest Landing? It has to be there," Madison said resolutely. "There's something I need to show you."

Silent hope rose in Ella.

Please, God, let her be willing to give the answers we so desperately need.

Ella saw Jude's jaw clench.

Her voice so low that Ella almost had to rely on reading her lips, Chen whispered, "Stall her."

"Give me an hour," Ella said. She knew the three law-enforcement officers in the room would want to come up with a plan.

"I can't wait that long," Madison said. "Don't tell anyone—especially not Jude. Or the police. My stepfather can't know."

"I'll be there as soon as I can," Ella said. "Just wait for me. I promise, I'll be there."

"I'll wait," Madison said with a tremble in her voice, "but don't take too long, Ella."

She disconnected.

Chen turned to Blake, who had been listening intently. "We need the chief out of the way. Find a reason to call him. Make it personal. A career question. Talk about a transfer. Anything. Distract him. Keep him on the phone as long as you can."

Blake's mouth flattened into a grim line. "I'm on it."

"Be convincing," Chen added. "If he catches even a whiff of suspicion, he'll be on the road before you hang up."

"I don't have a vehicle," Ella said.

Blake handed her his keys. "You'll have to take my truck. You can't show up in Chen's unmarked. Madison grew up in a law-enforcement family. She'd recognize it in a heartbeat. We don't want to scare her off when she's finally willing to open up."

Chen began to pace, her mind clearly working through every angle.

"Here's the plan. Blake, you keep Chief Zimmerman busy. Ella, you'll take his truck to the landing. Jude and I will go in my vehicle. We don't have time to wire you up. Maybe that's for the best. Anything official could tip Zimmerman off. We'll need to use your phone to record the conversation. Once you've got what you need, give a subtle signal. Scratch your head. Wave. Anything that doesn't feel forced. That'll be our cue to move in and bring Madison in for questioning."

"Bring her in?" Ella's stomach did a flip. "Why?"

"We'll still need a formal statement." Chen's expression softened. "I know Madison seems like a good person, and maybe she is, but she's connected to this, whether she realizes it or not. Remember, Ella, Jude's father is dead. And someone has tried to kill the two of you more than once. We need to question her officially. That'll go a lot smoother if she confesses to you first. It'll make it harder for her to backtrack or clam up. I'm also hoping it'll help me know exactly what questions to ask her."

Ella glanced at Jude.

"She's right," Jude said grimly. "You'll meet Madison as she asked, see what you can get out of her, but at some point, she's going to need to be formally questioned."

"We'll head out before you," Chen continued. "Give me a five-minute head start. I'll take the back road in and we'll position ourselves in the tree line for cover. I think there's an old logging area just north of the access. We can leave the vehicle there, then go in toward the access on foot. We'll provide backup."

"Backup?" Ella frowned. "Why would I need backup?"

"You probably won't," Jude said. "But I'm not risking this going sideways. What if Madison was part of the attacks on you?"

"No." Ella shook her head. She didn't want to believe it.

She may not have her memory, but she felt certain, down to her soul, that Madison was a victim in this, not a perpetrator. Regardless, she would feel better knowing Jude was nearby. And honestly, she thought he probably needed to be there. For his father. For closure.

"My ride's here," Blake said.

"What ride?" Chen asked sharply.

Blake headed for the door. "I called in a favor from someone I trust. Ella needs my truck, and I'll be more effective distracting the chief if I meet him face-to-face." He didn't wait for an argument. There wasn't time, and no one had one to offer, anyway, so he hustled out the door.

Ella caught sight of him jogging up to a burgundy SUV and he hopped inside.

The vehicle peeled away.

"Any questions?" Chen asked.

Too many, Ella thought. But none with clear answers. She just prayed they were finally about to get some.

THIRTEEN

The forest thickened with every bend, swallowing the road with creeping shadows. The freezing drizzle tapped against the windshield as Ella drove. She couldn't hear the wind but noticed the way the trees were swaying. The setting sun melted into bruised purples and deepening blues, the forest growing darker with every curve in the road.

Her fingers curled tighter on the steering wheel.

She wasn't sure if the ache in her chest was dread or determination...or both. She clung to the belief that God had a purpose in this chaos, that He hadn't abandoned them in the dark.

Jude had texted her moments ago, letting her know he and Detective Chen were stationed somewhere ahead in the woods. Madison was already there but they had managed to situate themselves without her noticing.

She whispered a silent prayer, the words ragged. *Please, Lord. Let this bring answers.*

But even at those words, a shadow of doubt crept in. What if this led to nothing? What if Madison clammed up again, or worse, lied? She wanted to believe that God was guiding this, that somehow justice would come from the ashes of everything they'd lost.

Guilt niggled at her, she didn't like the idea of deceiving Madison, yet this was too big of an opportunity to let pass by. They needed information and it was finally clear that Madison knew something…maybe everything.

When she reached the access road, she was reminded again just how desolate, how secluded, this area was. Blake's truck jostled over the rutted road, or path, really, as she curved through the woods. Then the path turned into an open, circular gravel area. As Jude had warned, Madison was already there. Her back was to Ella as she leaned on her SUV, looking out at the water.

The lake stretched before her, a sheet of blackened glass. Ella parked and then pulled out her phone and quickly hit the recorder app. When she opened the door, she was met by the eerie call of a loon. It echoed across the water, sending chills down her spine.

Pine boughs swirled overhead, caught in the gusty wind as waves crashed roughly against the shore.

Though the sleet had stopped, the air remained damp, heavy with the scents of wet pine and lake water. A thin glaze of moisture still coated the ground, turning the gravel beneath her boots slick. She didn't feel like the same woman who had once wandered antique shops and counted teacups. That version of herself—soft-spoken, hesitant, uncertain—was being stripped away by the day.

"Madison," Ella called as she approached, but the woman didn't turn to face her. Apparently Ella's arrival had been blotted out by the wind and the waves.

"Madison," Ella said again as she drew closer.

The younger woman turned. Something about her countenance seemed off. She looked stiff, unsure, her eyes… fearful. Anxiety rippled a warning down Ella's spine. She glanced toward the woods. Where were Jude and Chen? The logging trail was to the north so her gaze darted toward that tree line, but she saw nothing more than the thick foliage.

Yet, she knew they were there and that brought her comfort.

"Ella," Madison said, her voice trembling but loud enough to carry. "Can we just sit in my vehicle? We can talk there."

Ella nodded and stepped closer.

A man stepped into view then, emerging from the far side of Madison's SUV. He was tall, broad-shouldered, in his late twenties. He was good-looking in a rugged way, but looked haggard, like he hadn't slept or shaved in days.

For a second, she couldn't place him. But then, her stomach twisted and her heart gave a harsh beat.

She'd seen him before.

At Rocky's Café. He was one of the officers who had walked in with Chief Zimmerman.

He's a cop.

The realization struck her like a punch.

Was he the chief's henchman? Or was he the one who had left the note?

"It's about time you got here," he said, his tone hard. Sweat clung to his brow, and his jaw twitched.

Ella saw a flash of metal and realized he was holding a gun aimed at Madison. That's what had kept her there, pinned to the back of the SUV, which he'd been hiding behind.

Her gaze darted, almost instinctually to the trees again. Jude and Chen were to the north. They had seen that Madison was already here, waiting, but Ella realized that they likely hadn't seen this man, as he was on the south side of Madison's vehicle.

"What's going on, Madison?" she asked, trying to keep her voice from trembling.

Had this young woman set her up? She had thought they were friends. Though she couldn't remember, a friendship felt right. Had she been dead wrong about that?

"I'm so sorry, Ella. I didn't want to call you, didn't want to lure you here," Madison said, nearly sobbing. "But he showed up at my house, threatened my mom, then held a gun to my head and made me call you. I should've just let him shoot me."

The words splintered something inside Ella. Madison's fear wasn't feigned. It pulsed in her voice, in the way her arms hugged herself as if trying to keep herself from falling apart.

Madison hadn't set her up. She had no doubt. The woman was wracked with guilt. But wishing he'd just killed her?

No. Madison couldn't mean that. She wasn't ready to die, not like this. Ella's heart pounded harder. She couldn't let this end here. Not for either of them.

Ella blinked, disbelief and betrayal battling inside her as her mind whirled to figure out his part in all of this. "Who—who are you?"

"His name is Brad Nelson," Madison answered, her voice shaking. "He's a friend of my brother, Tate. He was there… the day the eagle was killed. The day Jude's dad died."

The flash of metal in his hand sent Ella's stomach lurching.

She had no doubt that Jude and Chen were well aware of this man's presence. She wondered if they could hear the conversation over the sounds of the rustling leaves and crashing waves.

"No time for questions," he snapped. "We've been waiting for you long enough. This is what's going to happen. You're going to get in and drive. I'm going to keep little Maddie in the back seat with me. You make one wrong move and—"

"He's going to kill us, anyway!" Madison blurted out, her eyes frantic and pleading. "He told me so. He was bragging that he's already dug two graves out in—"

"Shut up!" he roared as he gripped Madison's arms so hard she yelped. "Get in!" He tugged the back door open, but his eyes were locked on Ella. "No messing around or your friend is dead. And you'll be next."

Ella didn't doubt him. She fought to keep from scanning the woods for Jude again. Doing so might give them away. Both he and Chen were armed, but Brad—Officer Brad Nelson—had positioned himself close to the vehicle, with Madison on his outside, as if he instinctively knew he needed a human shield.

She reached for the driver's door, heart pounding, trying to think of a way to lure him away. Madison opened the back door just as Ella's hand closed around the driver's handle. The back door swung open and Madison hesitated.

Then, without warning, Madison turned, swinging her arm hard as Ella caught sight of a heavy metal thermos. It happened so fast she barely had time to process it. Madison slammed it into Brad's face.

He grunted and stumbled back.

"Run!" Madison screamed.

Ella didn't hesitate. She turned, preparing to bolt. But before she could move, Brad kicked her foot out from under her.

She went down hard, her knee slamming against the stones, her palms scraping through the wet grit. She scrambled to get up, but it was too late.

Brad lunged, grabbing the back of her coat and yanking her off balance. The cold barrel of the gun jabbed into her ribs.

"Move and I'll shoot," he snarled, blood now trickling from the corner of his mouth.

The metal burned against her side. Her heart slammed so loud she was sure she could hear it. She didn't move. Almost didn't breathe. She didn't dare.

Madison, who had nearly reached the tree line, whirled around.

"Get over here," he snarled at her.

Madison could have run off into the woods to save herself, but she stopped. Her expression twisted in horror as she realized Ella was the one in danger now.

"Get back here, girlie," Brad ordered. "If you don't, I'll shoot your friend. You know I will."

Madison took a tentative step forward, then another, clearly fighting her urge to flee. Her eyes met Ella's, so full of terror and apology.

But Madison wasn't the one who should be apologizing. This man, this traitor, should be.

"Madison, what's going on here?" Ella asked.

"He took the picture," she said, "after the eagle was killed."

"Shut up," Brad snapped.

"You were so proud of it back then," Madison went on, her voice shaking but strong. "You and my brother, Tate."

"I said…shut up!" His voice roared in Ella's ear. She felt the solid gun pressing against her back.

Jude…where are you?

Brad stood with his back to the vehicle. Even in her terrified state, Ella knew that neither Jude nor Chen could get off a shot without risking hitting her.

Ella's mind reeled. Madison had said her brother, Tate. So it wasn't her stepfather, Chief Zimmerman, who was responsible? Could he have been covering for Tate all this time?

Get him talking, she thought, struggling to pull together the right words. *Don't let this all be in vain.* Her hands trembled. Her knees ached from the fall. But she lifted her chin a fraction, just enough. If this was the moment God had been preparing her for, then she wouldn't waste it. Not now. Not when it mattered most.

Jude crouched low in the woods, heart hammering beneath layers of wet fabric. The wind howled through the trees, tossing branches like they were trying to tear themselves free. Autumn leaves swirled and crackled on the forest floor, covering the sound of his approach.

How could he and Chen have missed this guy? Neither of them had spotted him, on the other side of Madison's SUV. Guilt welled up in him. This was supposed to have been a simple meeting. Ella was to have a brief conversation with Madison, and then Chen was going to take it from there.

He should have insisted on doing the approach himself, even though he knew Madison would never confess to him. Still, he should've never let Ella walk in first. No matter how rational the plan had seemed at the time, it didn't matter now. All that mattered was the sinking knowledge that she was in danger. And he had let it happen.

It was not supposed to go sideways like this. Ella's life was not supposed to be in danger. He wanted answers, had yearned for them for so long, but not like this. His heart ached at the thought of the woman he loved being held at gunpoint.

This had to end.

Quickly.

He could hardly breathe. Every cell in his body seemed to be screaming at him to act, to charge into the clearing, to take a bullet if it meant getting Ella away from this man.

He recognized him, Brad something. He knew he'd been one of the officers at Rocky's. Had he left the note on the windshield? Probably. That was the least of his concerns right now.

Despite wanting to charge ahead, his training prevailed. He moved quickly and quietly forward.

Please, God, I love her. Always have, always will. Please, put a hedge of protection around her and keep her safe.

The prayer was one of sheer desperation, yet he had said it without hesitation. He loved Ella and it was ridiculous to try to deny that.

He caught sight of Chen as she edged to the north of the tree line, toward the entrance of the access. He crept silently toward the south. Toward the lake. Toward Ella.

She stood near the vehicle. Frozen, tense, her gaze locked on the man.

Brad's left hand waved aimlessly, but his right held a gun. And it was pointed at Ella, with the man's fingers twitching on the trigger. Jude's breath slowed, every sense on high alert.

He shifted, trying to adjust his angle, lining up the shot.

But the open driver-side door of Madison's SUV blocked his view, shielding Brad's torso and the gun entirely. If Jude fired now, it was a blind risk. The door would deflect the shot or worse…ricochet off it. And Ella was only feet away, with Madison not far off.

It was too dangerous from this angle.

The wicked autumn wind picked up, crashing the waves against the shore and drowning out most of what Brad was shouting. Though Jude strained to hear what he could over the gusts.

"Shot the eagle…" The wind picked up. "Panicked…" Another gust hit. "Cold blood…"

Jude's own blood ran cold. Was Ella recording this confession? She was risking her life to get answers. None of that seemed to matter now. His dad was gone, but Ella was here, and *she* was all that mattered.

He couldn't lose her, too. He'd lived through one horrific, life-altering loss already. It had hollowed him out in places he didn't talk about, even to himself. But Ella had filled those places back in with her love and quiet steadiness.

He crept closer. Almost there now. He couldn't see Chen as she moved through the trees, but he knew she would be closing in on them as well, coming in from the other side, the two of them performing a pincer move to apprehend Brad.

He was closer now, could hear more of what was being said.

Ella's voice rang out, pleading but strong. "You don't have to do this, Brad. You're just digging yourself in deeper. You can walk away from this. Walk away and not be a murderer."

Brad's hand jerked, the gun dipped, but then flew back into place. "Don't talk. I've had enough. Get in the vehicle! This ends now, tonight! I've lived with this shadow hanging over me almost my whole life and I just want it over with."

Without warning, a black Mustang roared down the gravel access road, engine snarling, tires spinning on the rain-slick surface.

The car skidded sideways into the lot.

The driver's door flung open.

Tate Zimmerman leaped out, his coat flapping, a gun already in hand.

"You moron!" he shouted at Brad as he stomped across the gravel. "What are you doing just standing there?"

Brad jumped, taking a step back. "I had it under control!"

"You call this control?" Tate growled. "You're letting them talk! Letting them stand there like you're hosting a tea party."

"What are you going to do, Tate?" Madison shouted over the wind. "Kill your own sister?"

He sneered at her. "I should've killed you, all those years ago, when I had the chance. I knew you were going to be a liability. You were a ticking time bomb. Get in the car!"

Madison shook her head and started to back away, though the lake was behind her and she had nowhere to go. With a snarl, Tate raised his gun…and fired into the ground by Madison's feet. The sound reverberated and gravel sprayed into the air.

She screamed, and staggered backward, crashing into her vehicle.

Jude's stomach turned to ice. He was almost there, so close—

And then, a single gunshot cracked from the trees. Tate cried out, stumbling forward as a bullet tore through his shoulder. The gun tumbled from his hand and bounced beneath the Mustang. He roared in pain, then gripped his wound and toppled to his knees.

Chen stepped from the woods behind him, weapon still raised. "Don't move!"

Brad spun toward the shot, distracted. His gun still pointed at Ella, but his focus shattered.

And that was all Jude needed.

He bolted from the woods, charging from the lakeside.

"Ella, down!"

She threw herself to the gravel, falling from Brad's distracted grip.

Jude slammed into Brad from behind.

They hit the gravel hard. The gun went flying, skittering into the puddles near the shoreline.

Jude grabbed Brad's collar and drove his fist into his jaw. Brad jerked, grunted, twisted and fought back.

"You killed him!" Jude roared over the storm. "You killed my father!"

Brad spat blood and punched back. "I didn't shoot him. It was Tate!"

Tate. Not Brad. But Brad had been part of it and Jude's emotions were running wild. His dad was dead and Brad had been there, had kept this horrific secret for all of these years.

They rolled, fists flying, knees slamming into gravel. Brad fought like a man who knew he had nothing left to lose. Jude fought like a man with over a decade of justice boiling in his veins.

Brad broke free, grabbing for something. A rock.

Jude tackled him again, elbowing him in the ribs, then jammed his knee into Brad's chest. The wind seemed to whoosh out of the man's lungs.

A cruiser flew into view, lights flashing, but sirens off. Then another…and another. The backup that Chen had called for the moment she spotted Brad had arrived.

"No more lies," Jude growled.

Brad glanced at the officers, his former teammates, who were now spilling from their vehicles, and he gave up the fight. He was defeated, with nowhere to go, and he knew it.

Chen strode across the gravel lot as an officer rushed to tend to Tate. Another trotted toward Madison.

"Here," she said to Jude as she held out a pair of cuffs to him. "I think you have waited long enough for this."

Brad sagged into the gravel, coughing, gasping and bleeding. Jude took the cuffs and slammed them onto Brad wrists, then stood and backed away.

He felt a soft touch grip his forearm.

"Jude?"

He turned to face Ella. Her eyes searched his. "Are you alright?"

"Yeah," he rasped out. "You?"

She nodded, looking unsure.

But when he pulled her into his arms, she didn't hesitate. Her body slumped against his, her arms tightening around him, and for the first time in a very, very long time, he thought maybe everything was going to be okay.

He pressed a kiss to the top of her head. He closed his eyes, breathing her in, blocking out the chaos around them.

FOURTEEN

The interrogation room was as uninviting as Jude had expected. Not because of the air exactly, but because of the way the gray cinderblock walls pressed in, stark and unwelcoming, like a prison cell dressed up as official business. A single utilitarian table sat in the center of the room, flanked by mismatched chairs and lit by an unforgiving fluorescent light overhead. In the corner, a small red light blinked on a mounted camera. Everything they said here was being recorded.

Detective Chen sat beside him. Across the table, Ella and Madison sat shoulder-to-shoulder, close enough for their arms to touch. Jude noticed the way Ella rested her hand on Madison's forearm. It was a quiet gesture of comfort. Protective, even now. Even without her memory.

Ella's gaze flicked toward him, catching his for only a moment, but he had to look away. His attention became hyperfocused on the phone sitting between them like a live wire. That phone held the key to everything. The truth. The end of a nightmare that spanned more than a decade. Tech had already pulled the audio and logged it into evidence. But the original recording still lingered on the device.

Waiting to be heard.

God, help me face this, Jude prayed silently. *I've been*

waiting for answers for so long, give me the strength to hear them.

His jaw clenched as he tried to steady his breath. He didn't know what it would be like to finally hear the words spoken aloud after eleven miserable years. Ella had tried to get Tate to talk. Now, it was time to hear what he'd had to say. Madison was here to fill in the blanks.

"Are you ready?" Chen asked quietly.

Feeling tense, Jude gave a sharp nod.

Chen hit Play.

Ella's voice came through first, the wind and waves distorting it slightly. Jude leaned forward, straining to hear over the storm on the recording. The wind gusted, the waves battered the shoreline, muffling the initial conversation. But then—finally—she asked the question that had lived in the back of his mind for far too long. *"Who killed Jude's dad?"*

"I didn't do it!" Brad's voice snapped out, frantic and raw. *"It was Tate. This whole mess is all his fault. He shot the eagle. He panicked when Warden Sheridan showed up. He shot him in the back when he turned to call it in. Tate knew killing an eagle was a felony. Knew he could go to prison and that there was a hefty fine. He panicked. But I didn't do it! I didn't kill him. Sheridan recognized him, knew his dad was a cop, probably trusted him enough that he never saw it coming. Never thought some young kid would shoot him in cold blood."*

Jude's stomach turned. Cold blood. That was how his father had died. Ambushed. His body just left there, at that deserted boat access. Madison's question cut through the static. *"Who decided to cover it up?"*

"You know who," Brad said, spitting out the words. *"Tate went to his dad. The chief, he was just an officer then, but he knew what to do. He called in a few news crews from a payphone. Said there was a boat holding a couple of teen-*

agers that capsized—a rescue going on at the landing. They showed up. The scene was contaminated, and he did what he could to subtly lead the department in the wrong direction after that. He worked his way up to chief to stay on top of things. He—"

The audio became distorted then—the chaos had begun when Tate had shown up at the lake, engine screaming.

Chen reached forward and stopped the recording. "We got what we needed."

Jude's throat was tight. "Is it enough?" he asked, barely able to get out the words.

"It's enough," Chen confirmed. "Brad gave a full confession to me before I came in here. I think he realized there's no getting out of this. He's hoping cooperation earns him a lighter sentence."

Ella leaned forward. "Is he the one who tried to kill me?"

His heart lurched at the blatant reminder that these boys, men now, had not only killed his dad to cover up the crime, but then had also tried to kill Ella as well.

"He is." Chen turned to Madison. "You're here because I'm hoping you can fill in the missing pieces. How did you come into possession of the Polaroid? Why did you bring the jewelry box to Ella's shop?"

Jude sat stiff, listening as Madison twisted her fingers in her lap.

"My mother had the Polaroid. I don't know how she got it, or when. I was going through her things one afternoon, just trying to downsize. It's likely she'll need to be moved to a memory care unit soon." She paused, swallowing hard. "She walked into the room and saw me holding the box. And she—she became extremely agitated. I asked where the photo came from, but she couldn't answer. She just kept repeating 'It's time to make things right.' That's when I brought the box to Ella's Attic. I told her…" Madison looked at Ella. "I told her you'd make everything right. That you'd fix it."

His gaze met Ella's and without saying a word, he knew she was thinking the same thing he was thinking. This is what Vivian was referring to when they'd visited looking for Madison. Vivian had said that Ella was going to fix everything.

Chen nodded. "That fits with what Brad said. He told me that while he was bringing a casserole to your mother, she became upset and told him he was a terrible, terrible boy. That he and Tate had done something awful. Vivian also said—" Chen glanced toward Ella "—that you were going to make things right. That's when he got suspicious. He started tailing you, Ella, weeks before the accident."

Madison covered her mouth. "I didn't know they'd spoken. Brad's always around our house. Our mothers are close but his dad left when he was a kid. He's always idolized the chief. They still shoot hoops in the driveway sometimes, even though Tate's had a place of his own for years. The chief has treated Brad like part of the family for as long as I can remember. He treats him more like family than he has ever treated me."

Because he liked Brad? Felt a sense of obligation since he was without a dad? Or had Chief Zimmerman taken him under his wing to keep an eye on him? To be sure he never told the secret that could utterly destroy the Zimmerman family? They may never know the truth, but Jude suspected it was the latter.

"Brad's mother sends meals over sometimes, so it's not unusual for him to be around." Her voice cracked. "I'm so sorry."

Ella shook her head. "You couldn't have known."

Chen's voice gentled. "Madison, we need your phone.

Brad admitted to installing spyware on it. He got access during a visit to your mother's house. After the conversation with Vivian, he began surveilling your texts and calls. He overheard your call to Ella. The one where you said you were ready to tell her the truth about the night Landon Sheridan died."

Jude's fingers curled against his knee, knuckles tight.

"That's the night," Chen said, turning her attention to Ella, "he ran you off the road. He's been after you ever since. Eventually, he pulled Tate in. It was Tate behind the wheel during the arson attempt. He drove the getaway car. Brad told Tate what he had planned for tonight. At first, Tate told him he wanted no part in it. Then decided it was in his best interest to provide backup, so he showed up late."

"Did you ever tell me the truth?" Ella asked softly. "Did we get a chance to talk?"

Madison shook her head. "I got called into work at the nursing home that night. Flu outbreak. We were short-staffed. We were going to meet in the morning, at your shop."

Ella nodded slowly. She hadn't gotten a confession, but she'd been close. Jude could feel it in her posture. She'd wanted to tell him. Chen had said as much. He believed, now, that she really was on her way to confess everything to him the night of her accident.

Jude found his voice again. "How long has your mother known?"

"I don't know," Madison replied quietly. "I don't think we'll ever have the answer. I assume she found the Polaroid and article somewhere. Probably hidden by Tate or Gus. I don't know when."

"And you?" Jude asked.

Madison blinked, lashes wet. Jude felt various emotions rise in his chest—betrayal, fury, heartbreak…all barely contained. He was furious with Madison for keeping this so long. He just wanted to understand why she'd done it. He needed answers, more than he'd been given so far.

"I was thirteen the night I overheard my stepbrother confess," Madison said. "It was late autumn. I loved the breeze, so I had my window open. I got out of bed when I heard voices. I knew right away it was Tate and his father. They were under the basketball hoop. Gus told him not to worry. That everything was handled. Said he'd disposed of the eagle, put it in a bag with rocks, dumped it in the middle of Shadow Lake, a much larger lake in the next county. He contaminated the Pinecrest Landing. Made sure no one would ever find viable evidence. Told Tate to forget the whole thing. That no one would ever tie it to him so there was no point in ruining his life over something he couldn't change or take back."

Her voice shook. "Tate looked up. He saw me. I was standing there like an idiot. Frozen."

Jude didn't speak. He couldn't. His chest felt too tight to breathe properly. But he didn't look away. Forgiveness didn't come easy. But hadn't Jesus said something about seventy times seven? Jude didn't feel like he had it in him. Not yet. But maybe the willingness to try counted for something.

"Later, I was lying in bed, a million thoughts going through my head. I didn't know what to do. Go to the police? Gus *was* the police. Then Tate came in. He didn't turn on a light, just sat on the side of my bed. I knew it was him. He brushed his fingers against my check, then I felt something cold, hard, sharp against my neck. I knew it was a knife blade. He said he knew I'd overheard, and if I ever told, no one would ever believe me because there was no proof, then he'd cut my throat wide open…and—" she choked down a sob "—my mother's, too."

"You never told anyone," Ella said.

Madison shook her head miserably. "Never. I tried to convince myself that I never heard the conversation, that the night had never happened. But I had nightmares for years, still do sometimes, and when I found that photo…" She shuddered. "I knew it was time. I finally had proof, something solid to go on, but I didn't know if it would be enough. I brought it to you," she said to Ella, "because I had recently joined Bible study and I knew you would know the significance of it. I didn't dare bring it to the station. Not when Gus is now the chief, not when Brad is an officer. I didn't know who I could trust. I suspected you were on to me, but I was torn. I knew no arrest had been made, and I started to wonder if the evidence wasn't enough. I wanted to tell you, but didn't know how. I was afraid I'd go to jail. Finally, I realized this had gone on long enough and I needed to tell you everything, then face the consequences."

Ella looked to Chen. "What are the consequences? For Madison?"

"Am I under arrest?" Madison asked, looking resigned to that particular fate.

"No," Chen replied. "Based on what we know, you haven't committed a chargeable offense. You're a material witness, not a suspect."

"But I didn't tell anyone," Madison whispered. "I knew what Tate and Gus did."

"In legal terms, failure to report isn't the same as obstruction or conspiracy. Unless we find evidence that you participated in the cover-up, you're legally in the clear. Emotionally? Ethically? That's something you'll have to work through. Sounds to me like it's something you've been trying to work through for a very long time."

"So I'm not going to jail?" Madison asked.

"No," Chen said. "But we need you to keep cooperating."

Jude, who had barely spoken since the recording played, finally asked, "What about Chief Zimmerman? I assume Tate borrowed the shirt from him and that the chief isn't the one in the picture."

Chen looked at him. "That's what I'm thinking. Regardless, Blake arrested him. Hernandez and Banks headed there right after leaving the access. Blake was still with the chief and they gave him the honors. He distracted the chief, just like he said he would. Zimmerman will pay for the part he played in this. Obstruction of justice. Evidence tampering. Official misconduct. He covered up a homicide his son confessed to. Destroyed wildlife evidence. Sabotaged the case to make sure it died."

Jude let out a long, ragged exhale. "So that's it. It's finally over, after all of these years."

Across the table, Ella shifted like she wanted to reach for him…but she didn't.

Jude's breath caught. His chair scraped against the floor as he stood.

"I've heard all I need to hear for now," he said. "I need some air."

Ella stood so fast her chair nearly toppled. "I'll go with you."

He held out a hand, as if to stop her. "Not now, Ella. Right now, I just need some time to myself."

As he stepped into the hallway, Jude whispered the only words he could manage. "Help me, Lord. I don't know how to move forward, but I want to."

It had taken every bit of Ella's resolve not to follow Jude out of the interrogation room last night. It had taken even more resolve not to go to his house afterward. The only thing that had really stopped her, was that she hadn't had a vehicle.

With everything going on, she hadn't even started to deal with the insurance claim after her accident.

Madison had taken her to the only car-rental place in town, where she'd finally gotten herself a vehicle to use until she got a replacement vehicle squared away. Then she'd spent the evening in her own home for the first time in days. Knowing Tate and Brad were behind bars brought her a sense of relief, not only for Jude, but also for herself.

Yet, she'd awakened this morning with Jude on her mind.

Armed with a box of his favorite éclairs, she was determined to find out how he was doing. Her breath caught when she drove past the skid marks her car had left a number of days before. She'd almost died here. If she had, would the truth ever have come out?

She turned into Jude's driveway. The long, gravel path was comforting and familiar. The horses grazing in the field lifted their heads in curiosity, but quickly went back to eating. When she pulled up to his house, she recognized Lexie's car, but not the other. The fact that it had Utah plates made her suspect it was Denise, his mother.

Doubt and hesitation hit her hard when she realized he had company. She should have called. It was presumptuous to just show up like this, thinking he might need her. Why would he need *her*? He had his family. They had never abandoned him, not like she had.

For a moment, she contemplated backing out of the driveway, hoping her arrival had gone unnoticed, but then Jude pulled the door open, probably curious about the strange car. She steeled herself—no going back now.

She would just deliver the baked goods, they were as good of an excuse as any, and be on her way.

After grabbing the bakery box, she opened the door, plastered on a smile and went to meet Jude.

"Hey," she said as she climbed the steps, "I'm sorry for just showing up. I should have called first."

"It's fine," he said. "Come on in."

Ella stepped into the living room where the scent of woodsmoke from the crackling fireplace lingered.

Jude's mom stood the moment she saw her.

"Ella," Denise said softly, her hand pressed to her chest. "You came."

"I brought éclairs," Ella said, lifting the box awkwardly, as if it could explain everything. "I wasn't sure if…"

Before she could finish, Denise had crossed the room and pulled her into a firm embrace. Ella stiffened, startled, but then leaned into the warmth.

"I've been praying you would," Denise whispered near her ear. "And not just for Jude's sake. We've all missed you."

Ella's throat tightened. "I didn't know if I should be here."

Denise pulled back, her eyes glistening. "You helped find the truth. That means more to me than you'll ever know."

"I still don't remember how everything came about," Ella admitted. "But I remember how much Jude meant to me. How much you all meant."

"Memory or not," Denise said gently, "God doesn't waste anything. Not pain. Not time. Not even confusion. Sometimes He brings us full circle so we can start again."

Ella nodded, blinking fast. "Thank you."

"You're still family, sweetheart."

Was she? She wasn't so sure.

From the hallway, a familiar voice chimed in. "Okay, okay. Enough with the warm and fuzzies already."

Lexie leaned against the doorframe, arms crossed, though a small smile tugged at her mouth. "I was prepared to glare at you the entire time. But…turns out I don't have it in me."

"I wouldn't blame you if you did," Ella said quietly. "I hurt your brother."

Lexie shrugged. "Yeah. But then you uncovered a cover-up, nearly got killed and still didn't run. That says something. You gave my family answers, and that's something no one else was able to do."

Ella glanced at Jude. He was watching her quietly from near the fireplace, one hand braced against the mantel, like he needed grounding. His posture was relaxed, but his eyes held something deeper. Exhaustion and grief still lingered, but he also carried a sense of relief. His family finally had the answers they'd been searching for.

Ella should leave them to each other's company. She didn't belong here anymore and was sure they had a lot to talk about.

She shoved the box of éclairs toward Lexie, who yelped in surprise, but took them.

"I should go. I don't want to overstay," Ella said as she met Jude's gaze. "I'm glad the truth is out. I'm so sorry for what I put you through. And thank you…for protecting me."

Still, Jude said nothing.

She turned toward the door, her chest tightening with each step.

But as she stepped out onto the porch, the wind caught her breath. The autumn air was crisp, the afternoon sun spilling through golden branches. Leaves swirled across the ground like confetti.

Was she doing the right thing? Was walking away what was best?

Then she heard the door open behind her.

She turned as Jude stepped outside, his boots silent on the worn planks. His jaw was tight, his eyes unreadable. But there was something else there, too. A light she hadn't seen in a long while.

He didn't speak. Just reached for her hand.

She let him take it.

Then he dropped to one knee.

Ella gasped, her heart stuttering in her chest.

From his pocket, Jude drew out the ring she had returned months ago. The same simple diamond he'd slipped onto her finger under a starlit sky long before everything had unraveled.

"I was just getting ready to come see you, when you showed up here," he said, voice husky. "I never stopped loving you, Ella Clarke. Not for a single second."

Tears stung her eyes.

"You might be missing months of memories," he continued, "but I know you haven't forgotten the years we spent loving each other before that. The way you looked at me. The way we fit. You came back into my life for a reason. And I think we both know what that is. God turns everything—even the hard, painful things—for good for those who love Him. He used your accident to bring us back together. I believe that. I believe in *us*."

She tried to speak, but her voice caught.

"I don't care how long it takes you to remember," he said, softer now. "I don't care if you never do. I just want to build something new with you. Starting now." He looked up at her, holding the ring. "Will you marry me?"

Ella's breath hitched. Her eyes burned. She wanted to say yes. Wanted to leap into his arms. But her mind flashed to Lexie and her fierce defense of her brother. Her warning. Her plea.

"I promised Lexie I wouldn't hurt you again," she whispered.

Before Jude could respond, the front door banged open.

Lexie barreled onto the porch, her cheeks flushed, eyes

wide. "Just say yes already!" she cried, exasperated. "We all know you want to!"

Ella laughed through her tears. "But what about the promise I made you?"

Lexie waved her off with a grin. "That was when I thought you were messing with his heart. Now, I know you were trying to protect him. Big difference."

Ella turned back to Jude, who was still kneeling, still holding out his heart.

"Then, yes," she said, voice trembling with joy. "Yes, Jude Sheridan. I will marry you."

A whoop came from inside the house as Denise grinned at her from behind a windowpane and clapped her hands with delight.

From the rafters of the porch, Bandit suddenly dropped with a disgruntled yowl, landing on the rail before twisting and looping around Ella's ankles as if approving her decision with reluctant affection.

Ella bent down, laughing, and scratched behind his ears. "Guess I have your blessing, too?"

In the nearby paddock, the wind picked up, rustling the brittle stalks of grass and sending leaves skimming across the fence posts. The old crew of geriatric horses lifted their heads as if sensing the shift. One gave a joyful whinny. Another pawed the earth.

Jude rose, and slipped the ring onto her finger once more. The fit was perfect. It always had been. The wind stirred around them like a whispered promise, and Ella knew—only God could take what was lost and turn it into something this beautiful.

EPILOGUE

Two months later...

The sun was setting outside of the church as snow lazily swirled down, leaving a light dusting on the freshly shoveled sidewalk. Inside, the sanctuary glowed with soft golden light. Red velvet bows decorated the end of each pew. Garland adorned each windowsill. At the front, just beside the altar, stood an enormous Christmas tree, its branches glittering with white lights and simple ornaments. Its quiet beauty added to the reverent stillness of the evening.

Ella stood at the window of the small room off the church's vestibule, her heart tapping out a happy beat of anticipation. Her dress, a delicate lace gown with a soft, flowing train, fit just right. Her heart fluttered as she thought of Jude, standing just beyond the sanctuary doors, waiting for her.

It felt almost surreal. She had dreamed of this day, then that fateful day last fall, had thought it had all slipped away. But when Jude proposed again, making everything in her world right, she knew she would never take for granted what they shared.

Her missing memories had not returned and she had come to terms with the fact that they may always remain a mystery. It no longer mattered. What mattered was the present, and her future, with Jude and the family they hoped to someday create.

Haven Creek was a small town, and thankfully, rebooking the church had been simple. The caterer had fallen through, but Ella managed to find someone from out of town and she could smell the delicious aroma of roasted chicken and herbed potatoes wafting in from the fellowship hall. Somehow, despite everything, the pieces of their wedding had fallen right back into place, as if it was always meant to happen this way.

"Are you ready, Ella?" Lexie's voice broke through her thoughts, and Ella turned to see her friend and maid of honor standing in the doorway. Lexie's smile was wide, her eyes sparkling with unshed tears. She was radiant in her bridesmaid dress. There was no longer any bitterness, no wall between them. Just the love of family.

Ella smiled, her chest tightening. "Absolutely. I feel like I've been waiting my whole life for this."

"My brother is blessed to have you," Lexie said. "We all are."

Ella blinked back tears, the weight of Lexie's words settling over her. "I'm definitely blessed. I didn't deserve him, Lexie. Not after everything. But he never stopped loving me."

"He never stopped loving you because you're worthy of that love," Lexie said firmly, her gaze steady. "We all have things we regret. We all have things we wish we could change. But one thing that never changed was your love for each other. And because of that, I'm so excited to be gaining the sister I always wanted."

Ella's heart swelled with emotion.

"Thank you," she whispered, her voice thick with gratitude.

Lexie smiled, brushing a stray tear from Ella's cheek. "I

mean it. I've never seen him this happy. And it's because of you."

The door creaked open again, and her two other bridesmaids, Julie and Stacey, stepped into the room, cheeks pink from the cold and excitement in their eyes.

"Final check is done," Julie said, brushing a snowflake from her sleeve. "The flutist is warming up, and your mom says everything out front looks perfect."

"And," Stacey added with a grin, "the girls are doing great. Little Emmaline is proudly guarding that satin pillow like it's a crown jewel, and Allie can barely wait to start tossing those petals around. Thank you for having my girls in your wedding. They're so excited."

Ella laughed softly, her nerves easing under their familiar presence. "I don't know what I'd do without you two."

Julie stepped forward, adjusting the lace at Ella's shoulder. "Probably show up without mascara, flower petals, or a ring."

Stacey winked. "That's why we're here."

They gave her quick hugs before slipping out again, leaving Ella and Lexie in the soft stillness of the room.

Before Ella could respond, the door to the room opened, and Jude's mother, Denise, stepped in, her eyes shining with pride and love. "Are you two ready?" she asked softly.

Ella's breath caught in her throat as she met Denise's gaze. She had always seen Jude's mother as a woman of quiet strength and unwavering faith. In the months that had passed since that fateful night at the Pinecrest Landing, she and Denise had grown even closer.

"Yes, I've never been more ready for anything in my life," Ella replied.

Her heart raced as she followed Lexie out of the small room and into the narthex. The church doors were already open to the sanctuary.

Just outside of those doors, her father was waiting for her.

Strong, though slightly unsteady on his feet, he stood tall in his suit, his expression full of love and pride. It meant everything to Ella that he was here today, stable enough to walk her down the aisle. He reached for her hand, squeezing it gently as she looped her arm through his.

Together, they walked down the aisle, toward her future. Toward the love of her life.

Ella's breath caught in her throat. She saw him standing at the front, his broad shoulders tense with anticipation, his eyes focused on her, as if he could already feel her presence before she even stepped into view.

Jude. The man who had waited for her. Who had loved her, even when she felt she didn't deserve it.

Their eyes met, and for a moment, the entire world seemed to disappear. It was just the two of them, bound together by something deeper than words.

Ella took a deep breath, her pulse quickening as she stepped forward with her father. Every step brought her closer to her future. She had no idea what the next chapter would hold, but she knew, with absolute certainty, that it would be with him.

At the front of the church, her father leaned in and kissed her cheek. Then, with emotion brimming in his eyes, he gently placed her hand into Jude's.

Jude's hand, warm and steady, found hers. He looked at her with such intensity, his eyes searching hers as if he was trying to read the unspoken words between them. His thumb brushed across the back of her hand, and Ella's heart fluttered in response.

"You're beautiful," he whispered, his voice thick with emotion.

As the ceremony began, Ella's heart swelled with a quiet

joy, the presence of God surrounding them, filling every corner of the sanctuary with peace. The pastor spoke of love, of faith, and of forgiveness. He spoke of the sort of love that was patient and kind, the sort that never gave up. It was the kind of love that she had found in Jude.

When the pastor pronounced them husband and wife, Ella felt a rush of emotion, a wave of peace settling over her. They had made it. They had overcome the darkness and danger, and now, they were stepping into the light, together.

And in that moment, as they shared their first kiss as husband and wife, surrounded by their loved ones and the glow of the season, Ella knew that whatever the future held, they would face it together with faith, love and hearts full of grace.

* * * * *

Dear Reader,

What do you do when everything familiar feels suddenly out of reach? For Ella Clarke, waking up with no memory—and discovering someone wants her dead—forces her to rely on the one constant she's always trusted: her faith in God. As she struggles to piece together her past, she learns that even when we don't have all the answers, God's plan for us is still in motion. We just need to continue to trust and let Him guide us. I hope Ella's journey encourages you to trust God's guidance, especially in the uncertain seasons of life. Thank you for joining her story of unshakable hope.

With gratitude,
Amity Steffen